# love **don't**
# **live** here
# no **more**

## Also by David E. Talbert

*Love on the Dotted Line*

*Baggage Claim*

## Also by Snoop Dogg

*The Doggfather: The Times, Trials, and*

*Hardcore Truths of Snoop Dogg*

book one
of **DOGGY TALES**

# love **don't** **live** here no **more**

a novel

## $\mathfrak{Snoop}$ $\mathfrak{Dogg}$ and
## $\mathfrak{David}$ $\mathfrak{E.}$ $\mathfrak{Talbert}$

**ATRIA** BOOKS

New York  London  Toronto  Sydney

**ATRIA** BOOKS

1230 Avenue of the Americas
New York, NY 10020

Library of Congress Control Number: 2006049886

ISBN-13: 978-0-7432-7363-3
ISBN-10:    0-7432-7363-X

First Atria Books trade paperback edition October 2006

10 9 8 7 6 5 4 3 2 1

**ATRIA** BOOKS is a trademark of Simon & Schuster, Inc.

Manufactured in the United States of America

For information about special discounts for bulk purchases,
please contact Simon & Schuster Special Sales:
1-800-456-6798 or business@simonandschuster.com.

For all our folks in inner-city black America . . .
whether that's where you grew up, got out, stayed,
or came back to . . .
our sincere desire is that this story, these characters, touch
your lives as much as they've touched ours.

# Snoop Dogg's Acknowledgments

There are so many people vital to my creative process, and I owe them for helping make this book breathe. Thanks to Ted Chung, Tasha Hayward, Nykauni "Nikki" Tademy, Shon Don, Chris Jackson, Stephen Barnes, Kami Broyles, GSO Group's Michael Oppenheim, Larry Tyler, and Sandy Cohen. To my crew at the Firm; Jeff Kwatinetz, my daily bread; Constance Schwartz; Kai Henry; Kevin Barkey; and my man with the books, Alan Nevins. Many nods-out to Dave Talbert, who made it real. And always, to my wife, Shante, and my children Corde, Cordell, and Cori for going along for the ride.

# David's Acknowledgments

Those of you familiar with my work are probably thinking the same thing I was when my agent first approached me about this project. But it took only one conversation with Snoop for me to discover that underneath all the hype and hoopla, some fact and some fiction, we have more in common than not. Both teachers, preachers, storytellers. I guess that's why it was so easy for us to work together. 'Cause really, whether you grew up in Long Beach, California, or Capitol Heights, Maryland, the inner-city black experience is a universal one.

Which makes this novel in many ways more than just entertainment, but a celebration of what's good and what's sometimes not so good when you grow up in the 'hood. It's a chance to reflect on real-life experiences through the eyes of some of the most interesting characters I've ever created.

I thank the Creator for bestowing upon me the gift of the written word. I honor it, am protective of it, and am humbled with each and every opportunity to share it. Thanks to my wife, Lyn, for always pushing me to step outside my comfort zone. And thanks for voicing over those vignettes on the single. You and Bootsy did y'all's thing!

Alan Nevins, my literary agent, thanks for making this project happen.

Constance Swartz, thanks for making the meetings happen—at least most of them.

Malaika Adero, thanks for pushing me to get this done.

Matt Johnson, thanks for always having my legal back.

To my creative collective: Mike Prevett, my Italian brother, thank you for always reading, re-reading, and re-re-reading my work. You're a godsend! Lolita Files, I could have never gotten through this without you. Every now and then God sends angels our way. I'm thankful he sent you and those homemade biscuits! Diondre Jones, my little brother and partner in crime. Okay novel!

**Acknowledgments**

Okay novel! You're the best. Thanks for keeping your big brother in touch with the streets. Laura "Little Momma" Reid, my tennis-shoe pimp—thanks for bringing your flavor and creativity to the think tank. You're up next! Thanks, Maurice "Bootsy" Wilkinson, for voicing over the vignettes and getting all your coworkers to proofread the manuscript. Morgan State, baby! Getting it done!

And finally to Calvin Broadus, aka Snoop Dogg, thank you for the collaboration. I've been a fan since forever. I'm now proud to call you my brother. Till next time . . . keep letting your light shine so that men might see your good works and glorify your Father in heaven. Let the chuuurcch say Amen. Amen.

And again, Amen!

**Acknowledgments**

# PROLOGUE

y heart was nearly beating out of my chest as I rushed down the stairs, racing with all of the strength that I had. The only father I knew. "Stay the fuck inside!" he said. "I got this." But there was no way I was gonna let him walk out alone.

*Fourth floor!*

This was my fault anyway. He was fighting my battles, making them his. What started out as a school yard beef between me and Chino had now become an all-out war.

*Third floor!*

I was dripping with sweat. All kinds of negative thoughts spiraled through my head. Maybe if I had never started selling drugs, none of this would have happened. I had to do something. Try to save him like he saved me.

*Second floor!*

"If it's gotta go down, then let it go down." His words echoed in my mind over and over.

**Love Don't Live Here No More**

Fuck that. If it's going down, it ain't going down without me.

*First floor!*

I was finally there. Nearly breaking my ankle, stumbling on a forty that had been left in the hallway. The rumbling sound of the elevator just arriving let me know I had made it before he did. The door leading to the garage hid my face as I cracked it, catching my breath, sneaking a look. As he passed, the scent of Drakkar trailed in the air.

The squeaking of his always fresh tennis shoes ended.

I waited a moment, preparing to follow. His truck door opened. Just as it did, I heard the sound of the mesh-covered steel garage door sliding back. Still behind the partially open door, I raised my hand to my eyes, blocking the glare from the oncoming headlights.

There was a sudden screech of tires. Voices shouted. Bullets began to fly.

Oh shit. It was going down.

More shots rang. Then there was nothing.

If it had to go down, it damn sure ain't going down like this.

From behind the door, I reached in my bag.

I had two Glock 9s.

It was time for me to use them.

**SNOOP DOGG**
**and DAVID E. TALBERT**

# CHAPTER

1

Hello, Ghetto.
To a son
to a motha

It was the eighties. The summer of 1989, to be exact.

Hip-hop was conscious. Rebellious. Stronger than the blackest cup of your mama's black coffee. Public Enemy was barreling through the airwaves. *"Fight the power. We got to fight the powers that be."* But no matter how much conscious rap we were listening to, niggas were still wildin' out, especially me and my brother Bing. Throwing bricks through car windows, crankringing doorbells, stealing candy from the corner store, and hanging out in the alley with baby hoodrats, lifting up their shirts and looking at their baby breasts, nipples shaped like Mike & Ikes. It's not like they were all that big, but to us they were winning. We were young and having fun. We were on one, living life the only way we knew. In the streets as much as we could be for as long as we could, or at least until somebody's grandmama came running out in her housecoat and pink slippers, chasing us away.

**Love Don't Live
Here No More**

"You see these damn streetlights! Don't make me come off this porch."

We were hoping to God that just one time she would come off the porch, but she never had to. In the 'hood, grandmamas were like the ghetto E. F. Huttons. When they spoke, cats listened. The Pro-Wings were hitting the asphalt.

Life couldn't get any better. And as bad as the world may have seemed to folks on the outside, from the inside, it was perfect. Even in the worst times, niggas still got their party on. Like the time Mrs. Johnson lost her job and got evicted, and Mrs. Jenkins threw her a rent party charging ten dollars a plate for some fried chicken, collard greens, and macaroni and cheese that didn't cost no more than two dollars to make. Or the time Mrs. Parker's phone got cut off and Mrs. Patterson let her get another one in her five-year-old son's name.

Shit didn't faze us, especially Bing and me. Not that we had a whole lot, but the little we had, Mama always made it seem like more. Like on birthdays. By the time Bing's rolled around, whatever I'd gotten on mine was rewrapped in a Broadway box with a stick-on bow and given to him. And those Christmases when money was tight, and we only got a Hot Wheel, some socks, and a pack of Fruit of the Loom. But by the time all the kids in the neighborhood played with each other's toys, it didn't matter, 'cause what one got, we all got. That was on the east side of Long Beach.

One day Mama came home with the bright idea to move us to North Long Beach, supposedly for something better. The way I saw it, though, North Long Beach rats were just as nasty as east side rats—they just breathed ocean air.

So off we went, looking like Arnold and Willis, cramming all our stuff into her dented-up, dingy blue Nova with a U-Haul attached to the back. The neighborhood kids were singing the theme from *The Jeffersons* as the car backfired out of one 'hood and into another.

"Here we are," Mama said, smiling and looking proud, like we had just pulled into Beverly Hills. Judging from the chipped stucco and barred windows; the liquor store next to the pawnshop next to the Nix Check Cashing Store next to First Baptist across the street from Third Baptist down the block from Second Baptist; Church's Chicken; and the older cats with the brown paper bags stumbling in the streets—instead of moving on up, we'd just moved over.

**Love Don't Live
Here No More**

We unloaded the one good couch covered in plastic that she would never let us sit on. It didn't matter who you were, you wasn't sitting on that couch. She didn't even sit on it. Next, we unloaded her favorite chair, the one place where she did sit. The tweed chair. The one that when you got up, it damn near scraped the skin off the back of your thighs and left an imprint on your ass. So old that the zipper was broken and yellow foam came out every time you sat down. She couldn't have been comfortable, but that's where she sat. And if you wanted to sit, that's where you sat, too.

Inside the apartment there was leftover gold shag carpeting from whoever lived there before. African beads dangled in the hallway. We had one bathroom and the hot water only stayed hot for ten minutes. Mama had the big room, which wasn't much bigger than the one Bing and I shared. At night you could hear the next-door neighbors threaten to kill each other, drunk on some cheap liquor.

"Bitch, I'ma kill you!"

"If I don't shank you first, you snaggle-tooth mutha-fucka!"

After that, the fucking began.

"Bitch, I'ma kill that pussy!"

**SNOOP DOGG
and DAVID E. TALBERT**

"If you don't, another nigga will, you one-tooth bastard!"

Bing and I could hardly sleep for the bedpost banging and more *"Yes, Lords!"* than in Sunday morning service.

Even with all that, Mama was still content with the move she had made, making us think it was hers, when really it was Grandma's.

"Blackdammit, Barbara, get them boys outta the east side," my grandma had said, pouring herself a little taste in her morning coffee. "'Cause if you don't, I will. These streets ain't nothing but a breeding ground for trouble," she continued.

It didn't matter what she said, "blackdammit" was always in there somewhere. It was her way of cussin', but not really.

No matter how we'd gotten here, we were here. And whenever I watched Mama pass by that one good couch so she could sit in that one bad chair, I knew that one day I wanted to get her couches, clothes, and whatever else she wanted as long as it was new.

Mama was our seventies soul superhero, still sporting a nappy 'fro fifteen years after the Black Power movement. She was hip, thin, and fine like she'd never had

**Love Don't Live
Here No More**

kids. My boys would make jokes about how sexy she was. Jokes that I never found funny.

Every Saturday morning she had us cleaning up the house to a never-ending eight-track tape of Aretha Franklin's *Young, Gifted and Black,* which by now we had memorized line for line. I would vacuum to "Rock Steady," Bing would sweep the dirt onto Earth, Wind and Fire's *All 'N All* album cover, while Mama would yell in the background, "Boy, don't you know that's The Elements?!"

Mama would sometimes pay us a dollar, but to get out of cleaning I'd give Bing a quarter of mine. Since he was five years younger, a quarter went a long way. I really didn't have to give him anything and he still would have done it. Bing was my man. He got his nickname from when he was two, running too fast, and he slammed headfirst into a wall. His head made a *bing!* sound when it hit. The way he bounced off it, we all thought his head had cracked open, but it didn't. He shot back up and staggered away. From then on, his name was Bing.

On the weeknights after work, Mama would come home, flip off her shoes, fire up the hibachi, and throw on some chicken wings, burgers, and links. It was like the Fourth of July weekend. Life couldn't be better.

**SNOOP DOGG**
**and DAVID E. TALBERT**

As we ate, she had the good sounds flowing through the house—Johnny Taylor, Betty Wright, and Tyrone Davis's "Turn Back the Hands of Time" was her favorite. We were dancing, singing, laughing, having a good time doing the Bump, the Rump, or whatever hot dances were out at the time.

My mom, Bing, and I, we were best friends. We were all we had and all we needed. She even let us get a little taste. She'd pour herself a glass of her favorite, Courvoisier, and leave the room and act like she was surprised when she got back and there wasn't none left. She knew what Bing and I were doing, but she didn't trip. And even our imperfect world where sometimes the light bill wasn't paid, or the window air-conditioner never blew cool air, or the busted pipe from upstairs stained our ceiling, was still perfect to us. We even had our own pet mouse named Ben. Ben would wait until two a.m. to race across the floor. Really he belonged to our neighbors by day, but at night he was ours. To us, life couldn't get any better. This was how it was supposed to be, at least in our minds.

That is, until one day Aunt Estelle came by with her crooked hat, matted wig, dress down to her ankles, and carrying a hundred-pound Bible. She wasn't really our

**Love Don't Live
Here No More**

aunt, at least not by blood. She was Uncle Donnie's wife, my mama's oldest brother. He had left her damn near the day after they got married, but we still called her our aunt. She had a strange look on her face. A look that let me know that shit was about to get all fucked up.

# CHAPTER

2

# Him and momma use to be cool

The music stopped and it never started back up. At least, not the kind of music we liked. You see, Aunt Estelle wasn't just saved, she was saved, sanctified, Holy Ghost–filled, and fire-baptized, with her mind made up and running for her life. And since she was saved, eventually so was Mama. Saved from what, I didn't know, because I thought she was safe all along.

We traded in Courvoisier for communion wine. Roberta Flack for Roberta Martin. And James Brown for James Cleveland. Our nights hanging out were now spent hanging in. No more playing, just praying. Now the only dance Mama was doing was the holy dance.

It wasn't so much the fact that we were going to church, because we were always going to church. You couldn't be around my grandmother and not know the Lord. But the God my grandmother knew was different

**Love Don't Live
Here No More**

from the one Aunt Estelle knew. Grandmama's understood the weakness of flesh, which is why she kept a shotgun in the closet and a fifth of Jack in the cupboard.

"'Vengeance is mine, saith the Lord,'" she would always say. "He gave us grace and mercy," she would continue, "but I'll give a nigga Smith & Wesson if I have to. God helps those who help themselves."

She was always twisting the scriptures to suit her needs. Especially if she had a drink or two in her. Her God was fun.

But Aunt Estelle had turned my mama into somebody we didn't recognize. We no longer knew her or the God she was serving. We started going to church five days a week. Monday night, prayer meeting. Tuesday night, Bible class. Wednesday night, missionary night. Thursday night we'd sit around the church trying to figure out what to call that night. Friday night, young people's night. Saturday, street meeting, where Mama dragged us out with Aunt Estelle as she walked up and down the neighborhood trying to convert people on the street. She was worse than Jehovah's Witnesses. At least when they came to your house you could close the door. You couldn't stop people from talking to you on the street.

Mean-spirited as Aunt Estelle was, I'm surprised

nobody clocked her in the back of her nappy wig with a forty of Olde E., although one time one of the cats on the street let his Rottweiler loose on her. Her Bible flew one way and her wig the other. It was the funniest shit ever. If it wasn't for my mama shooting us a look that said she was gonna whip our ass, we'd still be laughing.

Unfortunately, that was just an occasional break from the torture called religion, or at least Aunt Estelle's version that we were now being forced into. On the day that was supposedly for rest, we played musical pews from Sunday school to devotion service to morning service. We'd break for some fried chicken for lunch, then back to afternoon service. Break again for fried chicken for dinner, then evening service. Then a late-night fried chicken snack.

Bing and I were miserable. Life couldn't get any worse.

We had to learn the Ten Commandments, none of which we kept; the books of the Bible, Old and New Testament, none of which we cared about; and eternal life was the last thing either of us were interested in, especially if it meant Aunt Estelle was gonna be there, too.

We were no longer Mama's best friends. We had been replaced by Jesus. I knew she had to be missing

**Love Don't Live
Here No More**

Al Green because we sure were. But whether she was missing him or not, it didn't stop her from coming and going, going and coming, then coming and going back and forth to church. She was looking for something, something that Bing and I couldn't give her. But obviously Jesus could.

Since we couldn't find fun in the house, we had to find it somewhere else.

We were forced to find another best friend.

**SNOOP DOGG**
**and DAVID E. TALBERT**

# CHAPTER

3

**Break** the rules
*(why, why)*
As **time** goes by

It was 1990, the summer of crack cocaine, and not even Jesus Himself seemed to be able to save these smoked-out souls.

The neighborhood started to change.

Ms. Parker's hair, which had always been whipped, was now unkempt. Her socks were dingy, clothes dirty. The house where she used to throw rent parties to help bail people out of trouble was now a crack den.

"What are they doing in there?" Bing asked as we passed by, watching fools who looked like zombies stumble in and out of the black iron security door.

"Some shit that I better not ever see you doing," I replied, grabbing his arm and rushing him by.

Ms. Johnson's son, Fat Shawn, the neighborhood football star, had scholarships from almost every school in the country. He was six-foot-four, two-eighty, sporting the tightest fade in the neighborhood. Whenever you saw

**Love Don't Live
Here No More**

him, he had a wood brush in one hand for his waves and a bad bitch in the other. He started smoking that rock, and two months later, Fat Shawn was one-eighty with no scholarships. Two months after that, Fat Shawn was eighty, with a matted 'fro and a smoked-out strawberry with missing teeth, sporting her like she was a project princess.

Two months later, Fat Shawn was dead.

Businesses were closing one after another, except for the pawnshop where we saw crackheads carrying TVs, VCRs, boxes of Pampers, Nintendos, and anything else you could think of.

"Got them teef for five."

It was a crackhead that had walked up on me. He opened up his hand and in it was a set of dentures.

"They worth three hundred. Look at 'em, look at 'em, these a good set."

"Get out of here with that shit," I said, pushing him out of my path as Bing and I rushed past.

Crack cocaine was taking people out like you'd never seen before, and though my mama knew what was going on in the streets, she knew that her boys would never get caught up in something like that.

"That's the devil's handiwork, Barbara," Aunt Estelle

shouted. "Train up a child, Barbara, train up a child. That ain't nothing but a sin, an abomination all because Adam ate that apple. And the devil been cuttin' up ever since. Yes, Lawd! Yes, Lawd!"

Of course, I was curious about it. How did people lose weight so fast? It worked better than Dick Gregory. But the long-term effects were deadly. You'd see somebody one day and the next they'd be gone.

At night, staring out my bedroom window, I could hardly sleep. It was busier at night than it was during the day. The yelling. The cussing. The fights. Even the stench of crack smoke would sometimes seep through my window. After so many months of taking mental photos, one night I pulled out the piece of cardboard that was covering the crack in the window. I wanted the sounds from outside to come inside, raw and unfiltered.

All the *nigga, fuck you*s and the *kiss my black ass*. The street life. The life that my mama tried to shield us from. It was like I heard it for the first time. What I heard, I wrote about with my number two pencil. Not just that night, but the next night, too.

"Ulysses, whatcha doin'?" Bing mumbled sleepily as he weaved in and out of consciousness.

"Nothing," I replied. My pen kept moving and the

**Love Don't Live
Here No More**

words kept flowing until I ran out of cardboard and moved on to the wall by the window.

"You know Mama is gonna whip your ass for writing on the wall and she gon' whip mine too just so I don't get any bright ideas," Bing said as he drifted.

"Man, just go back to sleep."

Since he was probably right, I moved to writing on Mama's good napkins that she kept for holidays or when company came by. Not the cloth ones, but the thick paper ones that were the closest things to cloth her pocketbook would allow. Then, I finally switched to Mead college-ruled notebook paper. I wrote night after night, stuffing pages under my mattress. It was my way of escape. My way of making sense of the nonsense called life we were living.

# CHAPTER

# Gettin' women havin' money

**S**ummer had ended and I was about to turn sixteen.

I had reached that age. The golden age.

"When you gonna get some pussy?"

It was my boy Herc trying to clown me.

"I done already had some," I replied defensively.

"Who from, then?" Herc continued, drilling me.

"Yo mama, that's who," I said, causing Herc to start chasing me down the street yelling, "When I catch you, I'ma fuck you up!"

Truth be told, most niggas were lying on their dicks back in the day, so why should I be any different? And besides, fact was never as hot as fiction. Fools would spend hours lying on the dicks. Damn near came to blows arguing in defense of the lies they were telling. Sometimes they even started believing their lies were true.

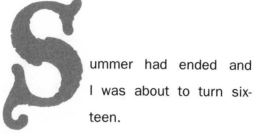

**Love Don't Live Here No More**

"I thought you said you fucked ol' girl last week," one dude would shout.

"I did," his boy would respond.

"But you said you fucked her cousin," another dude threw in.

"That's what I said. I fucked ol' girl *and* her cousin!"

We busted out laughing, knowing dudes were frontin', but it didn't matter. That's how it was on the block, especially when it was a lot of other cats around.

But when it was one-on-one with Herc, I really couldn't front. Herc was my man. My brother. We had been knowing each other since the first week Mama moved us to North Long Beach. He was a misfit, not really blending in with the crowd. Probably because his mama was always putting him on blast, putting his business out in the streets every time anything was wrong.

"Hercules Vernon," she would yell into the streets from her porch, "I know I just didn't look in your room and your bed wasn't made up." She'd continue, her hand on her hip. "You betta bring your ass in the house before I come out there and bring it in for you."

He was an outcast and I was new in the neighborhood, so it worked out for both of us. We had most of our firsts together. Saw our first titty together. Hit our first joint together. Had our first forty together. We were supposed to get our first piece of pussy together, but Herc swore he had gotten some first. I knew he hadn't.

"Man, I've seen more pussy than the free clinic," he boasted.

He was probably lying, but we really didn't care. It was gonna happen when it was gonna happen.

"Damn, who's that?" Herc whispered as a moving van pulled up to the apartment building down the block.

Climbing down from the passenger side was a light-skinned girl with freckles and a ponytail. She was wearing a miniskirt, showing more leg than the law allowed. She looked about our age, but developed. Had a body like a grown-ass woman. Thick thighs, breasts, and a booty you could rest your glass on top. We couldn't wait to get chose.

"That's me," Herc said as he tapped his chest.

"We'll see," I replied as we both stood there smiling, seeing which one she would give action to.

"See what I told you," Herc said.

"Hell no, I don't see, 'cause unless ol' girl is cross-eyed, she was looking at me," I said.

"You know what? Fuck you," he said, pouting.

"No, but how 'bout I fuck her," I said, as we watched

**Love Don't Live
Here No More**

her switch into the building, damn near popping every stitch in her skirt.

The next day we waited for her to come out, but nothing. The day after, nothing. Then on the first day of school, she appeared. I left Herc behind and followed after her, getting to her before anybody had a chance to spit game.

"Hey, what's your name?" I said.

"Mishi," she replied. "What's yours?"

"Ulysses," I said.

We continued walking for another block before either one of us said anything else.

"So where you from?" I asked.

"Lynwood," she replied as she sucked her teeth.

"So what grade you in?"

"Ninth," she said.

Ninth? *With a body like that?* I thought.

"What they putting in the water in Lynwood?" I replied.

"Oh, you got jokes. What you want to put in the water?" she replied, as she sucked slowly on her cherry-flavored Blow Pop.

I knew I hadn't had sex before, but by the way she looked at me like I was a T-bone, I knew I was about to.

**SNOOP DOGG**
**and DAVID E. TALBERT**

"Why you lying?" Herc said later.

"On my mama," I swore, lifting my hand to my chest.

"So what did you say after that?" he asked.

"I ain't say nothing," I replied.

"I'm your friend and you can tell me anything," Herc said. "But don't tell that to nobody else, okay? 'Cause if you do, niggas either gonna think you a simp, or that you scary."

"I ain't neither."

"When you ask a bitch what's in her water and the bitch replies with 'What you want to put in my water?' if that ain't an invitation to fuck, I don't know what is. Admit it, nigga, you scared."

"I ain't scared," I replied in a louder, more aggressive tone.

"Then why you acting bitch-made?"

"Cuz, ain't nobody acting like a bitch. I'm just a little nervous, okay?"

Herc could tell from the look in my eyes that I needed his help, so together we plotted the perfect time and place for Mishi and me to do the wild thang.

"Okay, man, don't fuck it up, alright?"

"Alright, why don't you stall me out. I can handle

**Love Don't Live
Here No More**

mine," I said, not wanting to listen to any more advice from a muthafucka who probably ain't had no pussy yet, either.

The plan was simple. I was cutting school right before gym and Mishi was supposed to meet me under the bleachers. The gym bell rang. I boned out, popped open the side door to the gym, and while everybody was outside doing track and field, I hid under the bleachers, waiting.

"You ain't scared, are you?" a voice whispered from the other end of the bleachers. It was Herc.

*What the fuck is he doing here?* I thought.

"Nigga, what the hell are you doing? She's gonna be here any minute," I whispered as loud as I could without being heard.

"Remember, there's two in holes and one out hole. Don't go in the out hole. And when she moves her tongue clockwise, you move yours counterclockwise."

Just as quick as he came, he was gone.

"Hey, baby."

It was Mishi. Skirt shorter than it was the first day I saw her. She reached for my belt and started to undo the buckle.

"I was thinking about you all day," she said.

She was like Houdini, popping open my belt faster than I could.

"I was thinking about you, too," I stuttered as she pulled my face to hers.

She opened her mouth. I opened mine. Was I supposed to move clockwise or counterclockwise? I couldn't remember, so I just followed her lead.

"You know this is my first time," she said as she pulled down my pants, then my draws, then down on her knees she went. Barely able to stand, all I could think was why the hell had I waited so long, 'cause this shit was the bomb.

She raised up.

"Did you like that?" she said, lifting her skirt and stepping out of her panties.

"Hell yeah," I said.

"Well, if you liked that, you gon' love this," she said, placing her hand on my shoulders, lowering me down, laying me on top of her.

I fiddled around for a while, then her hand replaced mine, guiding me in. Her hips started moving. Then mine. She started moaning, then I started moaning. Whatever she was doing, I was doing. It was like time had stood still.

**Love Don't Live
Here No More**

At least, for two minutes it did.

Like Mount St. Helens, I had erupted.

I rolled over.

"Wow. This is like I always thought it would be," she said. "I'm glad you were my first."

The bell rang for the end of the period.

I was official.

# CHAPTER

5

As **time** goes by

ext step was getting my driver's license. Not that I could really do anything with it. Asking for Mama's car was like asking for a kidney.

"Hell no, you ain't using my car!" she said. "I got one damn car and you ain't gon' screw that one up. Forgive me, Lord," she mumbled. "You damn near got me cussin'."

I guessed that was a no.

But I had plenty of other folks who would let me use their car, like my man Buddha, the neighborhood dopeman who had bank, broads, and Benzes. Buddha was big, black, and shiny, sportin' the flyest finger waves. His gear was always fresh to def—the dopest sweatsuits and spanking clean just-out-of-the-box tennis shoes to match. The jackets of his sweatsuits were never zipped all the way up, always open right above his bare fat belly and right below his three or four fourteen-karat-gold rope chains. On one of the thinner chains hung his Benz logo medallion.

"You can take the car and roll down the block, but if you fuck my car up, I'ma fuck you up," he cautioned as his boys laughed.

I didn't think he really meant it, but I wasn't taking a chance. He tossed me the keys to his 560 SEC, sittin' on chrome-plated Lorenzo rims with smoke-black-tinted windows.

"I know you ain't gonna drive Buddha's car," Herc said.

"Why not?"

"Why not?" he replied. "'Cause it cost more than both our mamas' salaries combined."

"You rollin' or not?" I asked.

"Not, nigga. Not!"

I popped open the door, hopped in the car, put my foot on the gas, and went as slow as I could.

"I could push the muthafucka faster than that!" Buddha shouted as his boys laughed. They were always cracking jokes on me, but I knew they were just testing to see if I could hang.

For some reason, Buddha always took to me, knucklin' up when he didn't have to. Like the time when Black Rob, the neighborhood bully, was picking on Bing and me, saying he'd had sex with our mother. Bing started crying, but I picked up a brick and busted him on the side of his head and ran.

Unfortunately, I didn't throw it hard enough because, seconds later, Black Rob was on me and would have damn near beat me to death, had it not been for Buddha.

"You wanna fight somebody?" Buddha said. "Fight me."

In the 'hood niggas knew who to fuck with and who not to, and Buddha was not the nigga to fuck with.

I didn't have a father or a big brother, so in a strange way, Buddha became both for me. He had the flyest crib in the whole neighborhood. From the outside it had Section Eight written all over it, but on the inside it was a mini-mansion. On the walls there were paintings of white people I'd never seen. Other than President Kennedy and the picture of Jesus that Aunt Estelle had Scotch-taped to the front of her Bible, I wasn't used to seeing shit like that, especially where we lived. He had the kind of furniture that you only saw in magazines. And there wasn't a piece of plastic anywhere.

**Love Don't Live Here No More**

Buddha even had a grand piano. Shiny black with a bust of a George Washington–looking cat sitting on top of it. His carpet was plush. You sank two inches every time you took a step. Each room had different color wallpaper. In the living room, he had big screens before big screens were big screens. Not like the wood-paneled floor model TVs that didn't work, that you only used as a stand for the little TVs that did.

And he had an aquarium. Buddha's fish were alive and colorful like the ones you saw on *The Undersea World of Jacques Cousteau*.

But my favorite spot in his whole apartment was the closet in his bedroom. It was not just a walk-in, it was a live-in, filled with walls of sweatsuits and shelf after shelf of unopened boxes of tennis shoes. A nigga could get his sleep on in there. Buddha was always bringing all the baddest freaks from the neighborhood up to his apartment, and he'd sneak me in the closet so I could listen. It was the perfect spot to hide.

"You're too young to watch," he said. "But you ain't too young to listen."

Buddha had more game than Colecovision. Smashing them one by one, night after night. They'd be giggling from the time they came in and knockin' boots 'til the time they rolled out. I was surprised the neighbors didn't call the cops as much his women would scream. But I guess having lived there so long, they knew that any pain they were hearing had to be good pain. Or at the very least consensual.

"That's gon' be you one day," Buddha said, standing in the doorway while his woman pressed the elevator button. "Yeah, that's gon' be you one day, loc. You gon' have all the bitches, and then some," he continued, quickly following behind her. Buddha always drove his females home.

He was like the king of the world to me. Somebody I wanted to be like.

Pretty soon he started letting me roll with him, making this stop here . . .

"What's crackin, Buddha?"

. . . and that stop there . . .

"What you holdin', cuz?"

I pulled out my pocket notebook and began writing what I saw. The reups that happened every other day. The strawberries who offered head for a hit. Every now and then he would take them up on it and sometimes make them do me.

"Fair exchange no robbery, loc," Buddha would

**Love Don't Live
Here No More**

say as he zipped up his pants, mashed on the gas, and bended corners. "What you writin' over there?" he asked, as he noticed me scribbling my thoughts. "What, you, five-oh or somethin'?" he said as he patted me down, feeling for a wire.

"Naw, man. I'm just . . . just writin' rhymes."

"Lemme see dat," he said, grabbing it out my hand. "Yo, loc, these ain't half bad." His eyes shot back and forth between the street and my words.

"Fa 'rilla?" I asked, pleased I had impressed him.

"Keep these close to the vest. I'd hate to have to peel a cap on a muthafucka for stealin' yo shit," he said. "And I *know* you know better than to put my name in any of this shit. 'Cause I'd hate to have to peel a cap in yo' ass," Buddha added, laughing but not playing. "Better get home, lil' homey. Jesus don't like it when you out after the streetlights come on." He chuckled.

I barely made it in before the streetlights. Mama was sitting in the living room next to Aunt Estelle with three or four Bibles open.

"He's running the streets, Barbara," Aunt Estelle said as she rocked in the chair. "Him and Satan. It's the devil's sanctuary out there." She shook her crooked finger in my direction. "Come here," she demanded.

**SNOOP DOGG**
**and DAVID E. TALBERT**

I turned in the opposite direction.

"Ulysses, you heard your auntie," Mama said. "Get your behind over there."

I reluctantly stood in front of Auntie Holy Roller.

"I can smell the foul stench of sin all over him," she said, sniffing the air around me. "And it don't smell good, Barbara," she continued. "Ever since Adam ate the apple, ain't been nothing but grief and ungodliness in the world. Train up a child, Barbara. Train up a child!"

While her lips were moving, my mind was spinning as I thought that it wasn't the devil that had gotten all over me.

It was Buddha.

# CHAPTER

6

Wanna be
# grown/out
on your own

**I**opened my eyes, staring at the unfamiliar sight of a Naka-michi stereo system that prob-ably cost more than our rent. Shit! I had fallen asleep at Buddha's.

I hopped off the couch, bust through the door, raced down the stairs, and shoved past the sea of OGs shooting dice on the steps in front of the apartment building. I hauled ass home.

Shit, she was gonna kill me. Or even worse, have Aunt Estelle beat more Bible scriptures into me.

I had never stayed out all night like this. But rolling up and down the streets, hanging out with Buddha with all his boys and all his women, I had lost track of time, and obviously time had lost track of me.

As the blocks got shorter, all I could think about was the fate that lay ahead. Not only had I overslept but I had missed school too, which was one thing Mama didn't

**Love Don't Live Here No More**

play. Education, in her mind, was the only way out. But what she didn't know was I had been getting a different education and, by now, getting out was the last thing on my mind.

As a matter of fact, staying in was just fine.

Finally I reached the door. *She's gonna kill me. I know it.* I slowly opened the door, hoping she wasn't home. No such luck.

"Where the hell have you been, Ulysses?" my mother screamed. "No child of mine should be coming in the house as I'm leaving for work."

"If I had an apple, I'd bust you in the head," threatened Aunt Estelle.

She was standing there in the background with her travel-size Bibles, obviously there to console Mama with a proverb, a psalm, or some fire-and-brimstone passage that would send me to the pits of hell.

"Where were you?" Mama screamed again. "Had me up all night worried to death," she continued.

"And had me up all night prayin'," Aunt Estelle added. "Train up a child, Barbara. Train up a child!"

Aunt Estelle stood with her hands in the prayer position, eyes clenched tight, face turned toward the ceiling. Her lips were moving fast without a sound coming out of her mouth.

"And had Winkie up all night, too. Having him drive all the way from Hawthorne."

*Oh, shit. Please tell me she didn't call Uncle Mike.*

"I told you his lil' ass wasn't gonna do nothing but get into trouble. You should have moved your ass to Hawthorne with me."

In from the kitchen walked the last person I wanted to see—Uncle Mike, Mama's bitch-ass younger brother. This was a grown-ass man who still went by the name Winkie, which Bing and I refused to call him. We figured a grown-ass man should be called by his grown-ass name.

Uncle Mike was thirty-five going on thirteen. Bing was more responsible than he was. At least every Saturday morning we cleaned up what we had messed up, but Uncle Mike would make a mess and leave it for everybody else to clean up. Mainly my mother. This nigga got more handouts than the Salvation Army. And like half the cats in the county, shit was never his fault.

"What's up, nephew?" Uncle Mike said, shaking his head. "You done really fucked up this time, huh?"

"Winkie, please," Mama said, cutting her eyes toward Aunt Estelle.

I wanted to slap the smirk off his face, but I couldn't,

**Love Don't Live
Here No More**

especially given the fact that I had been out all night. Uncle Mike always took up for my mama, which wasn't a bad thing, but in taking up for her, he was always tearing me and Bing down. Like us, he and Mama didn't grow up with their father, so he figured he would give us what he didn't have. Whether we liked it or not, he had appointed himself as the designated daddy. The only way he figured he could reach us was by accusing us of doing shit that we weren't even doing.

"And you made her miss work," he said. "You know we need this money." He paused, catching himself. "I mean, *she* needs this money."

"If a man don't work, he don't eat," Aunt Estelle chimed in.

"And I'm the man and woman working in the house," Mama said.

"How the hell you gonna make your mama miss work?" Uncle Mike added.

"The Lord don't like it when you miss work. Work or worship," Aunt Estelle continued.

It was like an orchestra, all three of them yelling at me at the same time. Finally the yelling ended as my mother grabbed her things.

"You stay your ass in this house, Ulysses!" she said,

pointing her finger between me and the floor. "You hear me? You stay your ass right in this house!"

"Yeah, keep your ass in this house and stay out of them damn streets," Uncle Mike said.

"Winkie!" she said. "Come on, Estelle. I'll drop you off at the church."

"Oughta knock you upside the head with this Bible, smelling like Satan's soldier. Train up a child, Barbara, train up a child," she mumbled as she and Mama left, leaving me and Uncle Mike alone.

"You ain't gonna do nothing but run the streets, end up selling drugs and getting these girls pregnant," Uncle Mike babbled on, searching for any negative stereotype he could find. Then he stepped to me, damn near nose-to-nose, sizing me up like he wanted to do something. But I knew he knew better than to put his hands on me. If he did, he was gonna get a designated ass-whipping.

"You just stay your ass in this house," he co-signed, walking out. "Like your mama said."

"We'll talk about this when I get home," Mama said from outside, shouting through the window, making sure everyone in the neighborhood heard her.

I knew what that meant: punishment. It used to mean an ass-whipping, but since I was older, Bing was the only

**Love Don't Live
Here No More**

one still at the age where he could get a beating. The last time Mama tried to whip me was a few years ago. It was one of those home-after-streetlights-came-on incidents. She raised up her hand and I caught it. We looked each other in the eye and both of us realized that an ass-whipping was no longer an option.

There I was alone, sitting in the house, bored as hell, staring out the window. Across the street, I started to see shit that I hadn't seen before. The neighborhood was a lot different during the day. There were things I'd never noticed, like the color of that building across the way. I'd always thought it was gray, but under the mid-morning sun, I realized it was really a dingy blue. Even the crackheads looked different, more toxic, with their patchy skin and ashy lips, sunken-in faces, twitching, fienin' for their next hit. I reached for my pad and began to jot it all down, inventing stories on how they got that way.

I saw Buddha's car roll past. As usual, folks flocked to the car like flies to shit, but this time it wasn't just hanging and talking shit or listening to the 808 sounds bumpin' from his Alpine. They were running up to the car, he was giving them dap with something in his hand, and they were dappin' him back with something in theirs.

**SNOOP DOGG**
**and DAVID E. TALBERT**

Damn. Buddha was making more money slangin' in the middle of the day than I ever saw him make at night.

I watched him all day long, parked outside across the street. Seemed like every five minutes somebody was coming to the car. He was handing them something, they were handing him something. All kinds of people, people I'd never expect to be coming over to Buddha. But I guess this was the best time to visit, when nobody was suspecting. Peeping Toms weren't watching because everyone was at work, and the kids weren't home so they couldn't tell their parents.

I saw Mr. Washington. He owned an auto shop on 53rd. I even saw Mrs. Thompson. She worked in the produce section at the grocery store. Damn, everybody was getting high and Buddha was getting paid. No wonder he was living how he was living and rolling what he was rolling. In addition to the cash, he was getting mad hook-ups, like fresh rims and a refrigerator full of food. He saw me through the window and motioned me out. If my mother came home and caught me outside, she was gonna whip my ass, or at least try to.

But what did I have to lose? I was already in trouble. Might as well make trouble fun.

**Love Don't Live
Here No More**

I eased out the back door, looked around to see if anybody was watching, then ran over to him.

"Lil' homey, what you doing home?" he asked.

"I fell asleep and missed school," I replied.

"Yeah, I figured you was gonna do that. Since you posted at the tilt anyway, you might as well roll with me."

I looked at the clock on his dashboard, figuring my mother wasn't going to get home for at least another five hours, and Bing for another three.

So I bounced.

We pulled off with Buddha's sound system blasting.

"Big things come in small packages," Buddha said, leaning in his seat, his eyes barely above the steering wheel. "See what you can do with this," he said, placing a small baggie in the palm of my hand as the car turned the corner.

I stared at my hand as the apartment building faded into the distance. I realized exactly what he was asking.

Buddha had just put me in the game.

# CHAPTER

# 7

# Coming up
## in the game/
### making a name

That bag stayed in my pocket for what seemed like weeks. I couldn't bring myself to ask somebody if they wanted it.

Even though I looked up to Buddha and admired the world he'd created, I never once saw myself slangin'. I had bigger dreams. My music was what I planned to put me on top. Selling drugs was the last thing on my mind.

Then Mama lost her job.

She was sitting in her tweed chair with the lights off when I came home, her hands folding and unfolding in her lap. That's what she did when she was worried. I knew right away that something was wrong.

"Mama, you okay?"

She nodded.

I kneeled down next to her, taking her hand. "No, you're not. What's the matter?"

**Love Don't Live Here No More**

She wouldn't look me in the eye. I could tell that she'd been crying.

"Mama."

"Not now, Ulysses. I need a moment, okay?"

"But what happened? Did somebody do something to you—"

She finally looked at me, squeezing my hand in hers. "They had to cut back at work."

"Mama—"

"It's alright," she reassured me. "I'll get another job. We'll be okay."

I could feel her hand shaking in mine. I gripped it tighter. "I can get a job," I said.

"No," Mama snapped, her face stern. Her hand wasn't shaking anymore. "You're gonna stay in school. That's all you and your brother need to focus on. We'll be okay. Now give your mama a minute to herself. I just need some time to think. Dinner's on the stove."

I wanted to say something to make her feel better, but I didn't know what.

"I love you, Mama."

"I love you, too, baby."

I kissed her on the forehead and walked away, glancing back at her.

Mama stayed in that chair for the rest of the night, long after me and Bing had eaten and gone to bed. She was still sitting in that chair when we got up the next morning. When she saw us, she went to the kitchen to make breakfast. She made our favorite, bacon, eggs, and pancakes. It was a feast we weren't going to see again for the next two weeks, as the money ran out and the food along with it. Oatmeal replaced meat for breakfast. Dinner ranged from fried sausages to sometimes nothing but buttered rice. The phone was ringing nonstop from bill collectors harassing us. Mama just stopped answering the phone.

Suddenly that package Buddha gave me began to have possibilities. I had to do something, even if it just meant getting decent food on the table.

It was the next morning. School had already been in for a while, so by now things were pretty settled.

Cats who thought they were gonna graduate but didn't were back. The ones who knew they couldn't graduate had left. We were sitting up in social studies listening to boring-ass Mrs. Rayburn talk about some shit that really didn't matter. All I was thinking about was that bag in my pocket, what I could do with it, and how much I could make.

Easing it out, I showed it to my boy Herc, who was sitting next to me.

**Love Don't Live
Here No More**

"Where you get that shit from?"

Herc was like me. We were in the streets but we were not really of the streets.

"You smokin' now?" he asked as Mrs. Rayburn raised her eyebrows for a moment, then continued.

"No, I ain't smokin'," I said, whispering. "I'm slangin'."

An *ese* in front of me cocked his head.

"This A-B, holmes," I said.

He turned back around.

"Slangin' to who?" Herc asked.

"Is there something you two would like to share with the rest of the class?" Mrs. Rayburn finally said. "Because obviously whatever you're talking about is much more interesting that what I'm talking about."

"You damn right," somebody mumbled from the back of the room. The class erupted in laughter.

"Please share, the rest of you keep quiet," Mrs. Rayburn said.

The bell rang through the hallway, saving us from having to respond. We had escaped and survived another confrontation with Mrs. Rayburn.

"You gon' slang it to who?" Herc asked, following me through the hallway.

**SNOOP DOGG**
**and DAVID E. TALBERT**

"Would you *shhh*," I whispered. "Talking all loud and shit. I'ma slang it to whoever wanna buy it."

"What you gon' do is go to jail," he warned, grabbing me by my arm. "And I ain't putting no money on your books, either."

"Ain't nobody going to jail, man," I said, shaking him off and continuing to walk, suddenly seeing the school and students differently. Before, these were just kids. Now they were customers, potential customers. People who I could come up on.

Then the day finally came. It was a Tuesday. We'd just been let out of an assembly and niggas were racing through the halls like roaches. The sea of bodies parted and there they were. I was looking at them and they were looking at me. These two dudes hanging in the hall looking like they had no intentions of going back to class. With nervous energy etched all over my face, I slowly reached in my pocket and pulled out the bag.

There it was. I didn't really know what was going to happen next. One of them slowly walked over. He reached in his pocket and pulled out a five. Our eyes remained locked as I handed him the miniature square neon-green Ziploc and he handed me the duckets.

It was official. I was now a dealer.

**Love Don't Live
Here No More**

# CHAPTER

Even if it's
**wrong,**
you gon' say
it's **right**

**B**uddha gave me two more baggies the next day.

Three the next.

Between math, social studies, and history, I was slangin'. I had bank. More fives and tens than Wells Fargo. In less than two weeks, I had at least twenty customers. I was getting paid. My pockets were swole. Even Herc peeped my game.

"Where'd you get that knot?"

"You know where I got it," I said.

Herc didn't mind what I was doing, as long as I didn't get in trouble doing it. Whatever I had I was sharing with him. While everybody else was eating the nasty cafeteria food, Herc and I were eating Quarter Pounders with cheese. We were living large, at least large on our level.

My life had changed overnight. I was walking a different walk and talking a different talk. I was *the muthafuckin' man.*

**Love Don't Live
Here No More**

Even Mama had gotten a job and was holding her head up high again. For the time being, everything at home was alright. Her being out of work was what had pushed me into the game, but the thrill of it all was what was keeping me in it.

Even Bing noticed the change in me. It was impossible for him not to. We shared the same room, the same dresser, and the same closet. If anybody knew what I had, he did. But more important, if anybody knew what I *didn't* have, it was him.

"Where you get that from?" he asked, looking at my fresh-out-of-the-box, blue high-top Filas.

"Why you asking so many questions?" I replied as I neatly laced them up.

"I just asked one," he answered, knowing the last pair of shoes we'd gotten had been at Christmas.

"Don't worry 'bout how I got 'em. You want a pair?"

Bing's eyes lit up.

"Yeah!" he exclaimed.

From that point on, I knew my secret was safe.

My mom had no idea what was going on. Trying to keep the lights on in the house and food on the table were enough for her to focus on. She didn't realize I was eating better than she and Bing were, and I was scared to let her know. Unlike Bing, she couldn't be bought off with a Fila T-shirt and a new pair of Guess? jeans. But maybe I could fulfill my dream of replacing her old couch with something better.

Everything was cool. Even an occasional visit from Uncle Mike and even more occasional visits from Aunt Estelle didn't bother me. Bing was cool with it, wearing the dopest gear and the flyest kicks. He couldn't wear them back home because Mama knew that she didn't buy them, so I would wait for him on the corner, pull out the blue Nike Cortezes, and he would change and wear them to school. Then I would meet up with him when he got out, he'd take them off, I'd put them in Buddha's car, and Bing would go home with his beat-up blue Chucks.

By now nobody was who they appeared to be. Not only Bing and me, but Buddha, too.

Buddha took me to his apartment and sat me down next to him at the piano. He was always playing some kind of classical shit that I had never heard before, but as unfamiliar as it was, he made it feel familiar.

He lit up a cigar. As the smoke ricocheted off the shiny black face of his grand piano, he said, "Whatever you do, do it with class. This shit don't last," he said, never once breaking stride from whatever the fuck he

**Love Don't Live
Here No More**

was playing. "Only one thing that's gon' last, and that's you. A true hustler always has another hustle. What you see is never all there is. The shit that I do is ugly. My job is to make it look pretty. Try to add some beauty to this shit," he said, still tickling the keys. "Try to give it some class. I don't just sell to anybody, but I sell to everybody. Niggas out in the streets just selling it to anybody, selling any kind of shit, they bring shame to the game," he said, lifting his fingers and turning to me. "Whatever the fuck in life you choose to do," he repeated, looking in my eyes, "do that shit with class."

He turned away and continued playing, taking puffs from his Garcia Vega.

"Now go on in the kitchen," he said, still puffing. "I got something for you."

I left for the kitchen, his words and smoke still swirling around me. On his marbletop counter, there was a Sony boom box with a red bow on it. Next to it was a microphone. Buddha didn't miss much. Rhyming was my dream. That other hustle. I guess that's what Buddha was just talking about.

Inspired, I rushed out of Buddha's apartment with the box and microphone. I couldn't wait to show it to Herc.

# CHAPTER

Him and
his momma
they got
a different
relationship

Fuck Kurtis Blow," Herc said, knowing that when it came to rhyming, Kurtis Blow was one of my idols. "LL, too. And The D.O.C."

*"Dammmn."*

We both looked at each other, realizing the magnitude of what he'd just said. The D.O.C. was West Coast rap royalty, a hip-hop legend in the making.

"The D.O.C.?" I asked.

"Yeah, I said it," he replied. "The D.O.C. If them niggas did it, why can't we?"

Now Herc was writing rhymes with me. From that point on, we spent every free moment penning verses, morning, noon, and night. We were on a mission. Before school, after school we were writing rhymes. Sometimes I could even talk him into skipping school so we could write some more.

Rhyming, slangin', and sleeping. That's all there was.

**Love Don't Live
Here No More**

Every now and then, Herc would come on a run with me. He'd act like he didn't want to, but anything I was into, he was going to at least check it out. He wasn't crossing the line to sell, though, no matter what kind of shoes I was wearing that he wasn't or how much cash I flashed that he couldn't.

"You know you ought to leave that shit alone," he said. "I ain't never seen Kurtis Blow rap from behind no bars."

Most of the time I shrugged it off, knowing he was just trying to protect me. But every now and then, he made me think. I still didn't stop.

Buddha stepped me up from selling nicks and dimes to selling ounces. I was the man, and everybody knew it. Even Mr. Wilson, the gym teacher, was a customer. I was doing my thing but, as usual, as soon as some niggas see other niggas coming up, that's when the tensions rise.

"So what, *vato,* you think you all dat?" Chino said.

That was Chino. An *ese* with a jacked-up grill who always rolled at least four deep. Him and his boys all looked like clones—white T-shirts; regulation khaki shorts that were four sizes too big, held up by a military belt with a gold buckle; Michael Cooper socks; and croaker sack slippers. They had Fu Manchu mustaches and their hair cut so close they were damn near bald. And locs. They all had locs.

Chino had been selling long before me. Word on the nigga wire was he wasn't too happy with the fact that some of his customers had switched up.

"Nah, I don't think I'm all dat," I said. "I'm doing what I do. I'm just handling mines."

"You servin' on my turf, holmes," Chino said. "Let me tell you something, *vato*," he said, posting up nearly inches away from my face. "*Pinche, cabrón,*" he said as his boys started laughing.

"If you gon' say some shit," I said, "say it in English."

"You want me to say it in English? No *español*? I don't give a *fuck* if you rollin' with Buddha or not. See, *pendejo,* a bullet ain't got no *nombre,* but I can give it one. *Comprende,* holmes? Was that better English?" he said, still inches from my face, pausing to make sure I understood what he was saying.

A threat was a threat, in English or any other language. I understood exactly what he meant.

Chino turned and walked away, motioning for his boys to follow.

I was unfazed. Like Buddha always told me, "Niggas

**Love Don't Live
Here No More**

fuck with you, they fuck with me. And don't nobody fuck with me."

With that said, I figured I was bulletproof.

Back on the streets it was business as usual. After school, Herc and I hung out. Writing rhymes. Writing scenes for our own music videos. We were destined for *Yo! MTV Raps, Rap City, The Box,* and anywhere else that would play us.

Even Moms was in a better mood. Every now and then, she'd slip on an Al Green record. But when she heard us come through the door, she would take it off real fast and replace it with some Shirley Caesar, *No Charge.* It made me feel better that she was at least getting some of her life back—the part that Aunt Estelle and *her* Jesus hadn't sucked out of her.

And Bing . . . Bing was geeked. Getting up earlier than me just so he could hurry up and get his old gear off and ready to change into some that was new. Yeah, things were popping off.

Until this one day I bounced from school headed over to Buddha's to settle him up, and I saw a crowd of people hanging on the corner. Pushing my way through, trying to see who it was, I finally caught a glimpse of Buddha's big hand mashed into the side of Chino's face.

"What your simp ass got to say now, 'holmes'?"
Buddha shouted as his fist crashed into Chino's eye.
"*Chinga tu madre,* muthafucka," he said, his foot stomp-
ing into Chino's ear, causing blood to squirt from his
nose. Buddha walked away, leaving Chino's beaten body
limp on the ground.

Word on the street was that Buddha heard that
Chino was mouthing off and chin-checked his ass for trying to move in on his turf. Obviously he didn't take that
too kindly. You see, the streets were like the jungle. It
was kill or be killed, eat or be eaten, shoot or get shot,
and if you got caught selling wolf tickets, your ass better
be able to back it up.

Chino's face was dripping with blood as his boys helped
him up. From the corner of the eye that wasn't shut, he
glanced at me with a look that said, *This shit ain't over.*

The crowd dispersed. Back at his ride, Buddha
handed his scuffed-up old Jordans to one of the BGs
that was standing by, popped open the car trunk, and
pulled out a pair of new Jordans. It was the first time I
had ever seen him or his sweatsuit dirty. He was covered
with blood, dripping with sweat. Usually he asked me to
chill with him, but he obviously had some other shit on
his mind.

**Love Don't Live
Here No More**

"You let me know if that buster fucks with you again," he said.

I nodded as Buddha hopped in the car and pulled off. Now I knew for sure the shit with Chino wasn't over. But still I wasn't worried.

Buddha just automatically did what he had to do for me. He was more than a father. He was a friend. If he hadn't put me in the game, I wouldn't have been able to do the things I was now able to do, like buying clothes for Bing and slipping an occasional twenty-dollar bill in Mama's purse on the low.

I rushed home, trying to hook up with Herc.

"Herc can't come out," his mother said. "I hope your report card is better than his," she continued. "As a matter of fact, Herc may never come out."

He was grounded. Again. To cats on the block, a bad report card was like kryptonite. It was the one thing with the power to bring the fun to a screeching halt. It wasn't that your mama expected all As and Bs, but she damn sure wouldn't tolerate Ds and Fs. It was one more thing to remind her that not only was she living in the 'hood but that her children weren't doing the best they could.

I learned early that the last thing you ever want to do is let your mama see your report card, so I made sure

mine got lost in the mail. By the time it finally did arrive,
Moms had so much other shit to deal with, like paying
bills and keeping the lights on, that my grades were the
last thing she was worried about. Especially since I kept
up the appearance of going to school and liking it.

"How's classes coming?" she said at the dinner
table as we ate her favorite, spaghetti and meatballs.

"They're coming along fine."

Bing chuckled to himself, knowing full well I was lying.

"You're not eating much," she said, noticing that I
had barely touched my plate.

"Yeah, Mama, my stomach's kinda hurting me, but
you know I'ma get my grub on later," I said, not wanting
to tell her the truth—that I'd grown accustomed to eating
out at restaurants with Buddha, so by the time I came
home I wasn't all that hungry. But hungry or not, I always
found a place for Mom's spaghetti and meatballs.

The night fell.

Bing had a strange look on his face, an unusual look.
Like there was something he wanted to tell me.

"Yo, what's wrong with you, man?" I said, cutting the
lamp on, tilting the shade to shine in his face.

"Nothing," he said, barely locking eyes with me.

"It's something."

**Love Don't Live
Here No More**

"Nothing, man. Stop sweatin' me," he said, even more irritated.

"Spill it," I said at his response, which had now confirmed my suspicions.

"I don't know if it's a good thing or a bad thing," he said softly.

"What is it? Just tell me," I replied, leaning up in my bed, now even more eager to know. "Bing, what is it?" I said in a stronger, more urgent tone.

"It's Mama. She met this dude at the church. He calls up sometimes and comes over when you ain't home. I don't know."

"What do you mean, you don't know?"

"I don't know," he said, even more bothered. "Something just don't seem right." Bing turned his back to me, pulling the sheet over his head. "It just don't seem right."

Another man in the house? In my mama's house? Shit, maybe I had been spending too much time away from home and not really peeping what was going on.

"Yo, Bing, don't worry about it, man," I said. "Ain't no man gon' come here and do shit in this house. I promise you that."

That was all Bing needed to hear, because whatever I said to him, he pretty much took as gospel.

I turned off the light and left the room, hoping Mama was still up. She was in the kitchen cleaning.

"Ain't it past your bedtime?" she said, looking at the clock on the wall.

"I was about to ask you the same thing," I replied playfully. "So I hear you met somebody. Trying to sneak a boyfriend around and not tell nobody?" I said, baiting her.

"When you start paying bills around here, Ulysses, then you question me about my personal life."

Whenever she threw bills in my face, I knew I had struck a nerve.

"Maybe I might not need to start paying bills. Maybe I can get your new man to pay 'em for me."

She stopped cleaning. Oh, I'd definitely struck a nerve.

"Ain't nobody paying for nothing up in here but me, understand? And so what if I do have a man, you got a problem with that? You jealous?" she said.

"No, I ain't jealous. I just wanna make sure if there is a new man, he's the right new man, at least right for you."

"Ulysses Jackson Jeffries, I think that's the sweetest thing you've ever said to me. Come here."

"Nah, Ma . . . "

"Come here," she called softly.

"Ma, I'm trying to have a conversation—"

**Love Don't Live
Here No More**

"Boy, come here!"

I dragged my feet as I walked over to her. She kissed me on my cheek.

"You know I love you," she whispered. "And you and Bing are the only men in this world who will ever matter to me."

Just hearing her say that meant everything to me.

We had a special bond. An unspoken relationship. Just the thought of her having a man other than us seemed odd. She had obviously been with men before, but we had never seen it. Sometimes at night we would hear other voices, and Mama always said it was the television, but Bing and I both knew better. We weren't like the other kids who had play uncles. Mama was private and kept her business her business.

Now she was getting her hair done every week. Buying new clothes. Taking extra long baths, leaving the whole house smelling like Jean Naté. The house was even cleaner than usual. Even Al Green made a cameo from time to time. Her spaghetti and meatballs started tasting different, not necessarily better, but like she was cooking it the way somebody else wanted it to taste, not us.

"Mama," Bing said, twisting his face up, "why the spaghetti taste funny?"

SNOOP DOGG
and DAVID E. TALBERT

"Boy, I been making this spaghetti like this before you were born! Talking to me about why the spaghetti taste funny. What we need to be talking about is them grades you brought home last week. All them damn Cs and Ds."

Bing never brought up the new and not improved spaghetti again, but the way Mama came at him only made me more curious about who it was for. So I started to do my own investigating.

I decided one night to surprise her by coming home a little early. But the surprise was on me.

"Ulysses, I want you to meet somebody," my mama said, blushing.

There he was, the new man, wiping spaghetti sauce off his cheek. He stood about five-nine, wearing a lop-sided Jheri curl with a dried-out rat tail, and a beard with specks of gray. He was short and ugly, looking like a cross between Ike Turner and Full Force.

"His name is Harvey," Mama continued. "Harvey, this is my oldest son, Ulysses."

It was a standoff, both of us holding our ground, neither one of us making a move. Then finally he reached out his hand, looking straight through me, letting me know he was in charge. I let it hang.

**Love Don't Live Here No More**

"Ulysses, Mr. Harvey wants to shake your hand."

I extended mine.

"Heard a lot about you," he said smugly.

"Heard nothing about you," I shot back.

"Yeah, well, we'll have to change that. Especially since I'ma be spending a lot of time with your mama," he said, putting his hairy ape hand on her shoulder, sliding it down past her elbow, pressing it into her hand. "That is, if that's alright with you."

"She grown," I said. "If it's alright with her, it's alright with me. But seeing that we only got two bedrooms, if y'all are spending time together, it ain't gon' be up in here."

"Ulysses."

"I'm just sayin', he's lookin' at me like he's runnin' something up in here."

"Ulysses, that's enough."

"Leave him alone, Barbara," Harvey said, sucking meatball out his teeth. "He's at that age where he's gotta push his manhood. Just know this, young man," he said, placing his ape hand on my shoulder. "Sometimes when you push manhood, manhood pushes right back."

From that point on, we understood our relationship.

We were at odds, fighting for the one woman who mattered: my mama.

**SNOOP DOGG**
**and DAVID E. TALBERT**

# CHAPTER

# 10

She got a man
in the house,
doing her own
thing . . .
it's a cold thing

harvey was dropping by every other day. Then every other night. Then every other day that led into every other night. Pretty soon I couldn't tell the days from the nights.

First it was an extra toothbrush that showed up in the toothbrush holder. Raggedy as it was, I knew it had to be his with barely a bristle left from brushing his ape-ass teeth.

His cheap-ass Aramis was funking up the damn bathroom. He really crossed the line when I opened up my dresser drawer and saw a pair of his dingy draws. Mama was obviously doing his laundry and got his draws mixed up with mine.

Then one morning I woke up and saw his bags in the living room.

This nigga had moved in overnight.

"You may not understand now," Mama said, as the

**Love Don't Live
Here No More**

steam from the shower poured under the bathroom door. "He's an important part of my life. Is there anything wrong with me having somebody?"

"Baby, get me a towel!" he yelled from the bathroom. "I'ma be late."

"Somebody, no," I said, watching her scramble. "But him? Hell no."

"What do you have against him?" she asked, reaching the towel inside the bathroom door. "Nothing, that's what. You're just used to having me all to yourself. You and your brother."

"No," I said, cutting her off. "I'm used to having some hot water left over so I can take a shower."

"What happened to all the hot water?" Harvey shouted.

"You used it up, that's what happened!" I said.

"Ulysses, would you rather share the hot water or not have any hot water at all?" she said. "Mama needs some help, and Mr. Harvey is willing to provide it."

"Is that all he's providing?"

She slapped me. Harder than she had ever slapped me before.

"Is breakfast ready yet?" Harvey yelled. "Want a man to work a full day, he's gotta eat a full meal."

**SNOOP DOGG**
**and DAVID E. TALBERT**

"I gotta fix Mr. Harvey some breakfast. Would you like something?"

She'd never asked if we wanted breakfast before. She just used to make it for us.

This nigga was in the house one night and already dining on demand. Shit was all messed up. It seemed like life as we knew it would never be the same. And neither would our relationship.

I didn't know whether it was the church, Aunt Estelle, or that Harvey was putting it down so hard, but whatever it was, Mama was a different woman. Bing noticed it, too.

"Want me to help you with your homework, lil' man?" Harvey would ask.

"No, thank you," Bing replied.

"You really oughta let me help you, man."

"I got it," he insisted.

"Obviously, you don't," Harvey said. "Grades coming in here C, C-minus, and Ds."

"Don't worry about his grades," I yelled from the back, overhearing their conversation.

"Somebody needs to worry about 'em," he yelled, matching my tone.

"Somebody. Just not you."

**Love Don't Live
Here No More**

He was butting into every aspect of our lives. All of a sudden Mama started cooking him special meals. Putting together combinations of shit that didn't even go together.

"Hey, Barbara, tonight why don't you hook up some macaroni and cheese, rice and gravy, some mashed potatoes, and some pork chops."

"Where the vegetables?" Bing said.

"If Mr. Harvey don't want no vegetables, Mr. Harvey don't have to eat no vegetables."

"But you always make us eat vegetables," Bing said.

"And what I should be making you do is your homework, instead of being up in grown folks' conversations."

"I offered to help him, Barbara," Harvey said.

No wonder why this fool stayed in the bathroom so long. He had to be constipated. He hadn't seen a vegetable in weeks.

Making matters worse, Sunday morning we were headed to church frontin' like we were a family. She met him in church and now she had to force him to go.

"Baby, I done worked all week long. I gotta go to church on Sunday? Shit," he said. "Can a nigga get some rest?"

"Yeah, well, the Lord gave you the energy to work all week. The least you could do is thank him on Sunday," Aunt Estelle added from the living room.

"I can't say it from the bed? Jesus Christ!"

"Thou shalt not take the name of the Lord thy God in vain!" Aunt Estelle said. "Say it again and I'll bust you in the head with this bottle of blessed oil."

"Get your ass up," I said, stepping into Mama's bedroom.

"Ulysses, don't disrespect Harvey."

"Oh, Lord, now you got the children cussin'," Aunt Estelle said.

"Ain't that taking His name in vain?" Harvey called out.

"He's disrespecting himself," I said to Mama. "And you."

"And God!"

"Let him go, Barbara. Let him go."

This was every Sunday morning. After church, I'd take a breather and call my boy Herc. He had gone through some of the same shit with his own mother, but even worse. In the last five years alone he'd had five different "uncles."

"Don't even let it get to you, man. Mom's gon' do what she gon' do and fuck who she gon' fuck."

**Love Don't Live Here No More**

"My mama ain't fucking Harvey," I said.

"What you think, they just slappin' bones? They slappin' alright, but it's some ass on that bone."

"Fuck you, Herc."

"No, he's fucking *her*. You gotta embrace that shit."

I wanted to kill him, but I couldn't. He was right, whether I wanted to admit it or not.

"Yeah, but why him?" I asked.

"Why not him? At least you've only got one to deal with. Imagine having five."

We laughed and drank and just for the hell of it, smoked up some of my supply. We damn near smoked a whole ounce that night, trying to drown our sorrows.

"Yo, man, what you doing this Friday?" Herc said. "We oughta go and hang out. G-Bang's gonna be at the club at a party that Chauncey's cousin Peron is throwing."

Chauncey was our homeboy from school. His cousin Peron was a local promoter. Every now and then, Chauncey would call us up and get us in the club for free. Even though we were underage, it didn't matter if you had the hookup.

"Shit, we ain't got nothing else better to do," I said.

Especially since Moms wasn't trippin' on me no

more because she was all up on Harvey's non-vegetable-eating ass. I was coming in after the streetlights came on, hardly ever checking in.

Friday rolled around. Herc and I changed into our freshest gear, mostly my gear and a few pieces we borrowed from Buddha. We rolled up into the Odyssey. Wall-to-wall bitches. The music was bumping.

"Yo, what up, U! What up, Herc!"

That was Chauncey, nodding and waving us in.

If this was how grown-ups kicked it, I couldn't wait to be an adult. This club was the bomb. Ass on top of ass. And dollar drink specials.

"What you want?" the bartender shouted over the music.

"What you servin'?" I returned.

We settled on Hennessy and Coke. We were already high, so the drink took our buzz to the next level.

"This is how it's supposed to be," Herc said, not noticing he was shouting way too loud. "That's supposed to be us. We're supposed to be up there doing that," he continued, pointing to G-Bang and his crew, who by now were onstage turning out the club.

*Yeah, right,* I thought to myself. G-Bang was the hottest thing in the LBC. Getting up onstage with him was

**Love Don't Live
Here No More**

what everybody wanted. But to me, that seemed like the untouchable, or at the very least the unthinkable. But Herc had extra-large dreams.

"Why not, man?" he said. "Somebody put him down. Why can't he put us down? We next, man."

"Yeah right."

"Nah, you gotta believe it. We next. I can feel it."

"Okay."

"Say it, man."

"Alright, alright, we next."

"Don't just say it. Say the shit like you mean it."

I did.

Just as it was starting to sink in, I turned around at the bar, reaching for another drink. Standing right in front of me was one of the finest chicks I had ever seen. Really, she was one of the finest chicks I had *never* seen, because she obviously wasn't from here. We had seen all the fine bitches in Long Beach, and she wasn't one of them. She had to be from L.A.

"You gon' get your mack on or you gon' stand there looking retarded?" Herc said, way too loud. "You scared?" Herc sniffed around me. "Just as I thought. Pussy."

"Ain't nobody scared."

"Nigga, you scared."

"Man, fuck you."

"No, man, fuck *her*."

I turned to take a quick breath check, gaining my composure, preparing to hit her with one of my patented mack daddy lines.

"Excuse me," I said.

"Excuse you? Do I know you?"

It was the voice of some other cat who had pushed up just seconds before me, cockblocking, taking my woman out to the dance floor.

"You think long, you think wrong," Herc said.

My eyes lingered, watching them get their groove on as G-Bang and his crew rocked the house. In my mind, I knew I had to see her again. And somehow I knew I would.

**Love Don't Live Here No More**

# CHAPTER

## 11

It's **crazy** how
love **changes.**
It's **amazing**

lysses, I swear, if you and Bing don't get your asses up! You gon' make me late for church," Mama yelled through our bedroom door.

Bing and I stayed in bed as long as we could just so we could make her cuss and use "church" in the same sentence.

"God don't like a lazy-ass nigga," Harvey mumbled while he chewed what was no doubt the last piece of sausage.

"You should know!" I shouted.

"Watch your mouth, Ulysses," Mama said.

"Leave him alone, Barbara," Harvey said. "He's just going through growing pains. One of these days, though, I'ma help his growth a little bit. Either that or his pain."

"You ain't gon' help shit," I shouted, making sure everybody in the house heard me. "And that better not be the last piece of sausage."

## Love Don't Live Here No More

"Ulysses!" Mama screamed. "I swear!"

"Swearing around the kids, Barbara," Aunt Estelle said. "Now you know better. Train up a child, Barbara. Train up a child."

We were at it as usual. I had to speak up, because if I didn't, Bing would have seen another man taking control around the house, and I couldn't let that happen. It was bad enough that another man was in the house, but I'd be damned if I was going to let him run it.

So there we were, crammed in Mama's two-door Nova headed to church, cussin' and fussin' all the way there. Mama and Harvey sat in the front, me and Bing in the back. Aunt Estelle sat between us, smelling like mothballs and peppermint.

"You want a mint, baby?" she asked, the plastic wrapper crinkling as she offered a piece of candy that looked like a mothball.

"Not if it smells like that," I replied.

"Ulysses!"

"That's alright, Barbara. The mothballs ward off the evil spirits. But he wouldn't know that swimming in Satan's cesspool."

"You got any Jolly Ranchers?" Harvey asked.

**SNOOP DOGG**
**and DAVID E. TALBERT**

"You need some Jolly Green Giant, you no-vegetable-eating bastard."

"Ulysses, I swear!"

"Train up a child, Barbara!"

Finally we made it to church. It was unusually packed this Sunday. The church was hot, the perfumes and colognes fighting for attention. By the time we made it to our seats, the preacher had just about finished his sermon.

"You done made me miss the message," Mama whispered into my ear.

Unfortunately, we hadn't missed the offering. In a black church they never took the offering early. They waited as long as they could to make sure everybody was there. Right after the altar call was the free will offering, then a song. The pastor's aide offering, then a song. The building fund offering, then a song. The preachers caught on early that if you kept black folks singing and dancing, they'd give you every dollar they did or didn't have. Mama reached in her purse for the little money she had and kept making sure that Bing and I had some to put in the tray each time it came around, even if it was just a little bit of change. She even gave Harvey's broke ass some money. A couple times I caught him trying to slip it in his pocket, but noticing my look, he begrudgingly dropped it in the tray.

**Love Don't Live
Here No More**

Everybody had a hustle in the 'hood, especially the preacher. He kept folks high on Jesus. So high they didn't mind that the preacher was living better than they were.

"If you give unto the Lord, He will surely give it back," the pastor would say.

But the way I saw it, wasn't nothing coming back. It was just going out—out of our pockets and into his bank account.

I sank in my seat, bored out of my mind, while the offering continued. Bing was feeling the same, playing tic-tac-toe by himself on the back of the church bulletin.

"The Lord loves a cheerful giver, amen," the pastor said, eyeing the tall buckets full of ones and fives. "Saints, we'd like to welcome our newest members into the church," he said. "Brother Henry Parker and his beautiful wife, Melissa, stand to your feet. Oh, and their lovely daughter, Aisha. Touch your neighbor and say, 'I was glad,' thank you, Lord," he said, wiping his mouth with his hankie, "when they said unto me, 'Let us go into the house of the Lord.'"

"Oh shit!" I accidentally let slip.

"Ulysses, did you just cuss in church?" my mother said, eyebrows raised.

**SNOOP DOGG**
**and DAVID E. TALBERT**

"He needs his ass whipped," Harvey answered.

Because of Aisha, I let that one slide.

"Both of you do," Mama said. "'Cause you ain't no better than him."

There she was. The girl from the club. In my church. This had to be a sign from God.

"What I say unto one, I say unto all," the pastor said in his usual benediction. "Greet our new members with a First Baptist hug, handshake, or a holy kiss, whichever one the Lord puts on your heart," he continued. "And Lord knows which one he put on my heart. And while you're at it, visit the missionary fund table and purchase you a piece of sweet potato pie and a fried chicken sandwich. Wheat bread is extra. Amen," he said. And the church responded with their own amen.

I nudged Bing, who had fallen asleep, and yanked him up to get in front of the greeting line. But by the time he did, there were at least a hundred people in front of us.

"I ain't waiting all day," my mother said. "If they're members, they'll be back next Sunday," she said, heading toward the door.

Next Sunday came, and by eight o'clock, Bing and I were dressed and sitting at the front door. Mama was

**Love Don't Live
Here No More**

shocked. There's nothing like the excitement of being interested in a girl with hopes that she might be interested in you.

The church was packed, but no Aisha.

The Sunday after that, a repeat of the same.

Finally, two Sundays later, there she was.

The sermon had ended and four or five offerings later, the church was letting out.

"Hurry up, now," Mama said.

"What about a slice of pie?" Bing asked.

"We got cake at home," Mama replied. "And it's free."

"And it's good," Harvey said.

"Thank you, baby."

"You're welcome."

It was enough to make me want to throw up.

"You know what, Mama?" I said, keeping a close eye on Aisha, making sure she didn't leave the church. "I'ma stay and, um, I'ma walk home."

"You gon' stay?" she said suspiciously. "In church?" she continued.

"Yeah," I said. "Is something wrong with that? I thought you'd be happy."

"What you up to?" Harvey asked.

"Don't worry about what I'm up to," I replied.

"Yeah, he's up to something, Barbara. We'll find out soon enough. 'What's done in the dark—'"

"That's scripture, you know," Aunt Estelle said.

"Let's go," Harvey said. "I'ma miss the game."

"You gon' be alright?" I asked Bing.

"You ain't gon' catch the holy ghost, are you?" he said.

"'Bye," I replied, pushing him toward Mama and Harvey.

Quickly I made my way to the back pew so I could catch Aisha before she left. Judging from her outfit, a blue skirt and white blouse, she had obviously joined the usher board. She began picking up fans from the front of the church, the skirt hugging her hips as she bent over, picking up fans one at a time. I wanted God to rain down fans all over the church so I could watch her pick them up.

She looked like that model on the box of *Just for Me,* her hair shiny black, her skin cocoa-brown, her cleavage parting her breasts like the mighty waters of the Red Sea. Can I get an amen?

She was the most beautiful girl in the world. At least in my eyes.

**Love Don't Live
Here No More**

I grabbed a handful of funeral home fans and held on to them with all my might, pretending to read the backs of them. I figured if I held on to a fan, she'd have no choice but to come and talk to me.

"Do you mind if I take those?" she asked, her lips as soft as a piece of Bubblelicious.

Looking up, I replied, "If you do, I don't know what might happen to me."

"What?" she said.

"Without these fans, I'm liable to catch on fire looking at you," I responded, slowly cracking a smile.

"Wow," she said slowly, contemplating my words. "That was the corniest line I have ever heard. Now can I have the fans?"

"If I can have your number."

"I don't give out my number to people I don't know."

"Then maybe you should get to know me."

"Keep the fans," she said. She turned and walked away. She didn't turn her head to look back. She knew I was looking at her ass.

The next Sunday, I was there again, this time dressed to the nines. Knowing I was up to something, Buddha had hooked me up with a suit. And this Sunday I brought some backup. My boy Herc.

"Why I gotta go?"

"'Cause if I gotta go, you gotta go," I said. "Just come on, man."

I was determined to have somebody to run interference for me, and Herc was the perfect one.

The service ended and while the pastor was pushing German chocolate cake and fried fish sandwiches, I pulled my mother close.

"Herc and I are gonna hang around for a minute. We're thinking about giving our lives to the Lord."

"And He might just give it back," Harvey said.

I swear, I wanted to slap that big-ass pair of front teeth out of his mouth.

"'Praise God from whom all blessings flow!'" Aunt Estelle exclaimed. "The prayers of the righteous, Barbara, they availeth much. Satan's playground has lost a playmate!"

I wasn't tripping on Aunt Estelle, either. I had more important things on my mind, and Aisha was all of them.

My mother gave me that look again, knowing I was scheming. Harvey, too.

"You can fool your mama," he said, "but you can't fool me. You're up to something."

"You gon' make me ride by myself with them again?"

**Love Don't Live
Here No More**

Bing said. "Why can't I stay here and give my life to the Lord, too?"

"You can give it to Him next Sunday," I replied. "'Bye."

Herc and I were sitting on the back pew, waiting for Aisha to come out and collect the fans. Almost half an hour had passed and no sign of Aisha. By now, they'd even run out of German chocolate cake and fried fish sandwiches, and still no Aisha.

"How much longer are we gon' sit here," Herc said. "I got shit to do. I mean, 'stuff,'" he said, looking at the picture of Jesus in the stained-glass window.

Just when we were about to leave, I heard a voice from behind.

"I see you brought your boyfriend."

It was Aisha.

"And you forgot something last Sunday," she said, handing me a fan before she walked away.

"When a woman hands you a fan, does that mean she's blowing you off?" Herc asked, laughing to himself.

I turned the fan over. To my surprise, her name and telephone number were written on it.

"Okay, I see you, I see you," Herc said, pounding me up as we both headed out of the church. "You think she got a sister?"

**SNOOP DOGG**
**and DAVID E. TALBERT**

# CHAPTER

# 12

He livin' wild . . .
He needs a
woman's touch

isha and I were talking all the time.

"I'm on the phone, Ulysses," Mama said. "It is *my* phone," she repeated.

Or at least we were trying to.

This was before the average cat had cellphones and two-ways weren't even a thought. Even if you did have a cellphone, that shit was so big, it was like putting a mini-refrigerator to your ear. There was no way you could hide it. And as nosy as Mama was, something that big would really catch her attention. Especially since she knew she couldn't afford it.

"I'm on the phone," Harvey said. "Ain't your mama taught you no manners, jumping in grown folks' conversations?" he continued.

Between Mama being on the phone with bill collectors and Harvey gossiping to his boys, I could barely get a call to or from Aisha. We didn't have call-waiting, or at

**Love Don't Live**
**Here No More**

least not the kind everybody else had. Mama's idea of call-waiting was if she was on the phone, whoever was calling had to wait until she got off.

But when I could get Aisha on the phone, we talked for hours.

It was young love. The New Edition "Mr. Telephone Man" kind of love. When it came down to a girl that you were into, it didn't matter how much street you had, you'd bitch up in a heartbeat.

I did all the kind of stuff you do when you first meet a chick and you fall in love. Or so you believed. Thinking about her all hours of the day. Calling her late at night, not wanting to hang up when you know it's way past both of your bedtimes.

"You hang up first," she'd say.

"No, you," I replied.

"No, you."

"Okay. On three, we gon' hang up. One . . . two . . . three."

Of course, neither one of us hung up.

We were falling head over heels. Ever since LL dropped "I Need Love," getting caught up was cool.

"You hit it yet?" Herc asked.

"What you think?" I shot back.

**SNOOP DOGG**
**and DAVID E. TALBERT**

"You ain't hit it," Herc said, looking me dead in my eye.

"Of course I did."

"How was it, then?"

"It was off the hook."

"You ain't hit that shit."

"Fuck you."

"No, fuck *her,*" he said, laughing. "I'm your boy. You ain't gotta lie on your dick to me."

"Why not," I said. "You lie on yours all the time," I replied, laughing even louder.

"Nigga, fuck you," he said.

"No, fuck her," I said as he started chasing me.

Maybe I hadn't hit it, but I was going to. I just couldn't let Herc know. Some girls you don't mind telling your boys about. How you hit it, when you hit it, how many times you hit it. But Aisha was special.

"Yo, that's a fly chick you got, YG," Buddha said, picking me up from Aisha's house after I walked her home.

"You plan on getting wet, make sure you got a coat. You got one, right?"

"Yeah."

"Where?"

**Love Don't Live
Here No More**

I didn't answer.

"Here," he said, noticing the blank look on my face, reaching in his pocket and pulling out a condom. "Use it. The last thing you need is one of these hoodrats holding you hostage. And when y'all do finally get down, since I know y'all ain't never got down, take her somewhere nice," he said, reaching in his pocket and handing me a couple of C-notes. "Don't just have her up in the back-seat somewhere or under the bleachers." It was like he could read my mind. I never told him about Mishi. "Show her some class. Take her somewhere nice. Take her out to dinner first. Buy her some flowers, something nice. Make it special. You'll remember her and she'll always remember you. And no matter how many times you fuck up, which you will fuck up, she'll forgive you for it 'cause you made her first time special."

From that point on, my mission was clear.

I wanted to make it special.

# CHAPTER

# 13

Some more
# drama.

Gettin' women,
## havin' money

hile Aisha and I were planning on making love, Chino and Buddha were plotting on making war. Shit had gotten heated in the streets.

What started out as simple beef had turned into an all-out vendetta. Chino's rep was on the line from that ass-whipping he'd taken from Buddha. In the streets, if you ain't got your rep, you ain't got nothing. He had *eses* posted up all over town. Buddha probably had more.

"On the 'rilla, you need to lay low for a minute," he said to me, "'til things cool off," he added.

I'd never seen Buddha like this before. I wasn't sure if he was worried for me or for himself. Either way, he was worried.

I headed out the next morning like I was going to school, but instead I hung out at Buddha's for a half

**Love Don't Live
Here No More**

hour, waiting for Mom and Magilla *Curl*'illa to leave the house. Then I turned around and went back home.

Since Buddha told me to lay low I started slangin' from my mama's house. Peeping through the window, I waited for my customers to hit the corner. I would meet them at the security gate of the building and there we'd make the transaction.

It didn't take heads long to find me, and pretty soon I had more customers out of school than I had in. But I wasn't selling just weed for long.

"It's time to step this shit up," Buddha said.

He opened up his bag and pulled out a little white vial.

"It's that hot shit. Sell it, but don't use it."

He didn't have to tell me twice. I already knew what it was doing to the neighborhood. Selling weed was one thing, but selling crack . . .

"Something wrong?" Buddha said.

"Nah, it's just that, you know, this shit is like . . . death."

"You wanna be Chuck D, or you wanna make some money? 'Cause right now rhymes ain't feeding you. It's supply and demand. If we don't sell it, somebody else will. Weed ain't gon' get that plastic off your mama's couch. Sometimes we do what we want to," he said, placing the vial in his car's cupholder, "and sometimes we do what we have to."

I picked it up.

Just like that, I was now a crack dealer.

**Love Don't Live
Here No More**

# CHAPTER

14

# Everything
## was
## everything

**F**inding new clients was the easy part. Getting to them was not so easy. Half the grown folks on my block didn't have jobs, so there were too many eyes starting to watch me. Like Crazy Betty.

"What you doin' down there, Ulysses? School on vacation?"

"No, ma'am," I said.

Actually Crazy Betty did have a job, but her job was at home. She watched special children. The state was giving her money to let them live in her crib. It was like a revolving door. Kids were always coming and going. There was always a short yellow bus in front of the house, picking them up and dropping them off. Her most recent two were Lorna and Leah.

"You know you supposed to be in school," she said, leaning over her balcony, which was one floor up and two doors over from our apartment.

**Love Don't Live Here No More**

"Yeah, I know. I'm just studying from home."

"Yeah, okay," she replied. "But when your mama finds out, she gon' be whipping your ass from home, to school, and anywhere else you done been or *ain't* been."

"Yeah, but that's *if* she finds out, right, Miss Betty?"

"I see your lips moving," she said, "but I don't hear nothing coming out. I can or can't see a whole lotta things, that is, if I don't want to."

From the look on her face, I knew exactly what she meant.

We called her Crazy Betty because she helped all the crazy kids, but she wasn't crazy at all. She had good sense.

We had an understanding. In the middle of the day, I'd to go up to her apartment and she'd fix me sandwiches in exchange for rocks.

She kept my secret and I kept hers. She even became my lookout.

"Hey, Harvey! How you doin'?" she'd yell from her balcony.

"I'm doin' alright," he'd say.

Talking real loud was Betty's way of letting me know that somebody who wasn't supposed to be coming over at that time was coming over.

"Yeah, you're looking good," she said, still talking to Harvey.

"Thanks," he replied.

"So how's Barbara?"

"Fine," he said, "but I'm in a rush. You take care now."

"Hell, sometimes I be in a rush, and I ain't got nowhere to go."

She continued to talk long enough for me to grab my shit and slip out the back.

Then there was the time that bitch-ass Uncle Mike came over.

"Hey, Mike! How you doin'? I like that outfit."

Uncle Mike had on a dark blue satin short set, some long black dress socks, leather sandals, and a black fanny pack.

"You do?" he replied.

"Not really."

By the time he got inside, I was down the block and around the corner.

"Hey, Miss Estelle! How's things down at the church?" Crazy Betty would shout.

"Oh, fine. Blessed and highly favored. Walking in the light. You ought to come visit us some of the time."

**Love Don't Live**
**Here No More**

"Yeah? If some of the time is none of the time, I'll be right there."

Crazy Betty had jokes that were not just funny, but long enough for me to make a clean getaway. We were a good team, thanks to a never-ending supply of crack and fried fish sandwiches. If it wasn't for her, I would have been busted a long time ago.

As for my homework, well, that's what Herc was for.

"I ain't gon' be doing this shit forever."

Herc was smart. He just acted stupid. Since I was always cheating off his work in class anyway, it didn't make much difference for him to just go ahead and do my homework for me. During the day he was keeping up my front in school and at night we were making beats. In addition to the boom box and the microphone Buddha had given me, I bought Herc a Casio drum machine.

"Man, this is hot," he said, "but you know I can't take this shit home. If you think I was on punishment about my grades, if she see me come up in her house with some shit she know she ain't bought, you might not ever see me again. Why? 'Cause she gon' take my ass straight down to juvie herself."

I was leading many lives. Dealer by day . . .

"Let me get that rock."

**SNOOP DOGG
and DAVID E. TALBERT**

. . . aspiring rap artist by night . . .

"You supposed to be writing rhymes."

. . . brother . . .

"I thought you said you was gon' buy me some shoes?"

. . . son . . .

"Ulysses, I swear!"

"Leave him alone, Barbara."

"Train up a child."

. . . and boyfriend . . .

"How come you ain't call me last night?"

I was on autopilot, being whoever I needed to be whenever I needed to be it.

That was my life, and as crazy as it was, it was about to get worse.

**Love Don't Live
Here No More**

# CHAPTER 15

The way she raised him . . . No one could faze him

**I**t was seven a.m.

I woke up to constant banging at the front door. Shit. I was about to get busted by one-time. I jumped out of bed, scrambled for my shit.

"What's wrong?" Bing asked, as I snatched open dresser drawers, flipped my mattress, and tore through my closet for the rest of my stash.

"Damn, Barbara," Harvey shouted. "That church woman's coming over on Monday?"

I raced past her bedroom door to the bathroom.

The banging continued.

"Her name is Estelle," Mama said. "Are you gonna get the door?"

I was on my knees. Hand shaking, sweat pouring.

"I don't wanna go to jail. I don't wanna go to jail."

"This ain't my house. Why I got to get the door?"

I flushed a handful of vials. They all popped back up.

**Love Don't Live
Here No More**

Shit.

I was going to jail.

The banging continued.

"Never mind," Mama said. "I'll get it myself."

I heard the squeak of her mattress, the stomp of her feet. Her bedroom door opened.

The bathroom door opened.

Fuck going to jail. Mama was going to kill me.

I turned.

Bing handed me a small Ziploc bag half filled with water.

"Put 'em in here. This'll make 'em go down."

I did as he said. It worked.

Mama walked past the door looking worn and frustrated in her pink chenille house robe covered with flowers and head full of yellow plastic curlers.

"Ulysses, I swear," she said, giving me a sharp look. She paused. "What the hell are y'all doing?"

Before I could open my mouth, Bing said . . .

"Cleaning."

"Uh-huh," she said under her breath.

The banging continued.

"This door better not be for you," she said, looking at me. She walked away.

As we followed her into the living room, Bing shot me

**SNOOP DOGG**
**and DAVID E. TALBERT**

a look that said there was no need to discuss what had just gone down.

Mama looked through the peephole, then at me. She sighed, unlocked the two sliding chains, the dead bolt, and the lock on the knob. Slowly the door creeped open.

"Hey, big sis!"

Aw, hell no. I had just flushed all my shit for no reason. Bing and I shot each other a look.

It was Uncle Mike standing with two suitcases and a look on his face that said this was more than just his usual drama. Something that a meal, a twenty-dollar bill, and a pat on the back weren't going to solve.

*Shit. Buddha's gonna kill me,* I thought.

"Hey, Winkie," Mama said. "What's going on? This is early for you."

"Early for me, too," Harvey shouted.

That was at least five hundred dollars' worth of crack. Somehow I was going to have to make up the loss. Whatever Uncle Mike wanted better be worth it, or he was gonna get at least two times that much worth of an ass-whipping.

Uncle Mike could smell an opportunity. Like the time my mama got a bonus from her day job when she was working at the bank. It was five hundred dollars, money she had

**Love Don't Live
Here No More**

planned to get some new curtains with. Here comes Uncle Mike. He needed a new exhaust pipe on his car. There went the five hundred dollars. Or the time she got an unexpected refund from the IRS for four hundred dollars, enough to pay three months' rent with money to spare. Here comes Uncle Mike, claiming he got his girlfriend pregnant and didn't have money for the abortion. There went the four hundred dollars.

Mama must have gotten a bonus or a refund check I didn't know about. Either way, if she did, it was about to be gone.

"What's up, nephew," he said.

"You don't even wanna know," I said, wanting to stab him in his neck.

Mama cut her eyes, sending me to my room, but Bing and I kept our ears pressed against the door trying to overhear the conversation.

"You ain't in trouble, are you?" she asked.

"I'm sorry, sis, but if it wasn't important you know I wouldn't be here."

"At seven o'clock in the morning, it better be."

"I lost my job."

Bing and I looked at each other, both shaking our heads.

"The place where I was staying said if I didn't come up with the three months' rent I was late on, I had to leave. So I left."

We both knew what was coming next.

"I'm not trying to inconvenience you, sis."

"It's not an inconvenience."

*Like hell it ain't,* I thought to myself.

"Of course you can stay here. We're family," Mama said. "And it couldn't be at a better time because you know I just got a raise."

I knew it.

"Big sis, that's the best news I've heard in weeks," he said. "But where I'ma sleep? You already cramped up."

Like he really cared. We all knew he was just saying that to cover up what an inconvenience he really was. We seemed to be in the middle of an epidemic of sorry-ass men. First Harvey, now Mike.

"Bing and Ulysses got a room. I guess you could stay in there," she said.

"Aw, hell no!" I shouted through the door.

"I heard that, nephew," Uncle Mike shouted back.

"I hoped you would," I replied, opening the door and walking toward them.

"Yo, unc, we at capacity already. You know we only got two bedrooms, and one of them's already got one freeloader we don't want up in here."

"Shut your mouth, Ulysses," Mama said, "or I'll shut

**Love Don't Live
Here No More**

it for you. You're right. We've got two bedrooms that you don't pay one penny for," Mama continued. "Now you show your uncle some respect."

"First he gotta show us some respect, Mama. We barely got enough room here as it is. It was tight before you moved Harvey's ass up in here."

"Leave me out of it, nigga," he shouted through the door. "And could y'all lower your voices. I'm trying to get some sleep."

The circus had come to the ghetto. Mama was the ringmaster. We already had an ape and now we were about to get a clown.

"Sis, I really don't want to put you out."

"It's too late for that," I said.

"You got a problem with me, nephew?" He called Bing and me both "nephew."' Not as a sign of affection, but for real, I don't think he knew our names. So to keep from making a mistake, he just kept it generic. "'Cause if you do, just say it, nephew," he continued. "Don't beat around the bush."

"I wasn't beating around the bush," I said. "I'm trying to chop it down so it don't keep growing."

"Ulysses, you got one more time to disrespect your uncle. Now say you're sorry."

"But I'm not," I said.

**SNOOP DOGG**
**and DAVID E. TALBERT**

"But you're gon' be if you don't say it," she replied in a tone that let me know she wasn't playing.

"Look, sis, I'm not trying to cause any more trouble for you, your boys, or your new man. But I'm in between a rock and a hard place. Shit, for real, fuck the rock, I'm just in a hard place. If you could see fit to give me a roof over my head for a few days, I'd appreciate it. Just until I get back on my feet."

He might as well be walking on his ankles because he was never on his feet.

Mama paused, then they hugged.

"You know I love you, little brother. Anything I can do, I will. Ulysses, get your uncle's bags."

"You can't be serious."

"I am."

"But, Mama, we only got two beds."

"Your Uncle Mike will sleep in Bing's bed. Bing can sleep with you."

"How Bing gon' sleep with me," I shot back. "It's a twin bed!" I continued, not believing what I was hearing.

"So act like he's your twin since you wanna be a smart-ass."

"I ain't sleeping in there," I said. "I'ma sleep on the couch."

**Love Don't Live
Here No More**

"You ain't sleeping on my couch. I got one good couch, and you ain't gon' mess that one up."

"Well then, I'll sleep on the floor. The place where he *should* be sleeping."

"Suit yourself," Uncle Mike said.

Ain't this a bitch? "Suit yourself.'"

"Winkie, you hungry?" Mama said.

"I could use something to eat," he replied.

"So could I," Harvey shouted. "I coulda used some sleep too, but since y'all done woke me up, you might as well feed me."

As tired as Mama was, she went right into the kitchen and made breakfast for not just Mike, but Harvey as well.

Bing and I stood in the doorway watching Harvey and Uncle Mike tear through a pack of sausages, four stacks of pancakes, French toast, a half-dozen eggs, a pot of grits, and a gallon of orange juice to wash it all down. It was the battle of clown versus ape.

"Winkie, I'll see you when I get home," Mama said. "If you need anything, here's my number at the job. Just call me."

"Alright, brother-in-law. Make yourself at home. If you need anything, you call her," Harvey said, patting him on the shoulder, then leaving.

Ain't this a bitch? He's telling *another* nigga to make himself at home at a home that wasn't his.

Mama and Harvey left.

Bing and I went to the room to get ready for school. We passed Uncle Mike on our way out the door. He was sprawled out on Mama's one good couch with his shoes on.

"If you need some help with your homework, let me know."

"Did you graduate from high school?" I asked.

"Nah, but what's that got to do with anything? Neither have y'all."

Bing looked at me, shaking his head.

"So what you gon' be doing here all day, Uncle Mike?" I asked, thinking that he had to be out of the house because he was going to interfere with my business.

"I ain't doing shit, nephew. I'm in between jobs."

"In between jobs, like you got one job somewhere and another job somewhere else?" I asked, already knowing the answer.

"Very funny," he replied. "You know what, nephew," he continued, "all this food and excitement done made me tired. I'ma go to my room and take a nap," he said,

**Love Don't Live
Here No More**

walking past Bing and me to our room, where we heard

him kick off his shoes and flop on the bed.

Again Bing looked at me, shaking his head as we walked out the door, realizing our home would never be the same.

**SNOOP DOGG**
**and DAVID E. TALBERT**

# CHAPTER

# 16

You put your **brother** in danger, you put **me** in **danger**

s usual, Bing and I made a pit stop in the alley to change. Bing reached into my bag, pulling out a fresh pair of tennis shoes and new shirt. I did the same.

"You know those new Jordans come out on Tuesday," he said.

He knew I would get them, especially after what he'd done for me that morning.

"How long you think he gon' be there?" Bing asked.

"Hell if I know," I said.

"I hope not long, 'cause I don't think we can fit on that one bed."

"Yeah, well, we gon' have to," I said.

"Well, see you later," Bing said, making his way from the alley as he headed off to school.

Bing didn't worry about too much. He wasn't carry-

**Love Don't Live
Here No More**

ing the same kind of emotional weight or responsibility that I was. To him, change was normal. To me, normal was a change. Like Harvey being around. Other than the obvious, like the fact that he ate up all our food and used up all the hot water, Bing didn't really know why it was such a problem to me. I remembered Mama and Daddy being in the same house, being in love. Taking showers together. Listening to the eight-track, dancing in the living room. I remember them fucking on that one good couch, which was why she probably had plastic on it in the first place. And even though Mama thinks I don't remember, I do. I was six when our father left. Bing was just one.

With Bing headed off to school, I was faced with my biggest challenge yet. Not only was I having to deal with Harvey and now Uncle Mike, my office was now occupied. And I needed to settle up with Buddha what I had flushed away. I was in between selling a rock and finding a hard place to do it.

I was standing in front of my apartment building trying to figure it out.

"Gon' be pretty hard selling candy if somebody's up in the candy store," Crazy Betty said, peering from her balcony. "That is, unless you got another store that'll sell it for you," she said.

I knew exactly what she meant.

I had just found a new partner.

But first I had to deal with the partner that I had.

Buddha.

**Love Don't Live Here No More**

# CHAPTER 17

# He said he's makin' paper

**y**ou think I'm stupid, lil'
nigga?" he said with a
gun barrel shoved in my
mouth, the cold steel grinding against my teeth. "You
think you the first muthafucka who done told me some
shit like this? Where's my fuckin' money?"

This was the Buddha I had never seen, at least not
directed toward me. It was the same Buddha who had
stomped Chino.

"I thought it was the cops, I thought it was the
cops."

"What you say, you thievin' muthafucka?"

My words weren't clear. It's hard to talk when you've
got a gat in your mouth.

The gun slid out.

"What the fuck you say?"

A tear slowly fell from my eye.

"I would never do that shit to you, Buddha. You gave

me my boom box. You gave me my mic. I wouldn't do that to nobody, especially not you."

Buddha walked away without saying anything.

Seconds later, he was back with a new Ziploc bag full of vials.

"Make my shit back," he said, dropping it on the table in front of me. He walked over to his piano and sat down. Before I could respond, he began playing some of the darkest shit I had ever heard.

I was dismissed.

I walked around the corner and into the back of the apartment building. I went up the stairs to Crazy Betty's, where I began to set up shop. For the next few days that turned into the next few weeks, there I was, selling candy from my new candy store. Downstairs, Uncle Mike was still at the spot, never, ever leaving the house. In between jobs? Hell, he wasn't even looking for a job. *And* he snored.

As inconvenienced as I was, I had to stay focused. I had to keep the main thing the main thing, and the main thing was moving enough product for Buddha so that he wouldn't think that I was slacking. My problems were my problems. I didn't make them anybody else's, especially Buddha's. He had been nice enough to not only put me on, but keep me on. The last thing I wanted to do was add any more pressures on top of the pressures that he was already dealing with.

"Here's three now," I said, handing Buddha a knot of money with a rubber band around it. "I'll have the other two next week."

Things were changing. Not only with me, but with Buddha. For the past few weeks, he wasn't acting the same. When I would spend time over at his apartment, all he did was play the piano and he hardly ever talked. He was even drinking more. Making runs by himself. He had even picked up some extra runners that, to me, seemed more like bodyguards. He was never alone. Everywhere he went, they went. Whenever he drove, there were at least three or four cars behind, like he was the president and they were members of the Secret Service. Usually when I walked into the room, he didn't mind me sitting in listening to the conversation. Now they would stop and wouldn't start back until I left. He was planning something, and whatever it was, it was something he didn't want me to know about.

It probably had something to do with Chino. Word on the street was he hadn't learned his lesson from that first ass-whipping Buddha gave him.

**Love Don't Live Here No More**

At school, Chino had taken most of my customers, and out on the street he had even moved in on some of Buddha's. I was surprised that Buddha hadn't taken him out, but I guess he knew something that I didn't. I trusted that whatever it was, when it was time for me to know, I would.

It had been weeks since I had talked to Aisha. Not for lack of trying, and I hoped not for lack of her wanting.

She had one of the few families in the neighborhood with a mother and a father who cared about what she was doing and who she was doing it with, so on her end things were pretty different.

"My mama said I can't be on the phone all night," she said, whispering. "And my father's starting to look at me funny every time the phone rings. I think we need to take a break," she continued, which was the last thing I wanted to hear. She was just about the only thing going right in my life, and I'd be damned if I was going to let anybody or anything fuck it up.

"A break from what?" I asked.

"You know," she said.

"No, I don't," I replied.

"Aisha!" It was the sound of a grown man's voice, probably her father's.

**SNOOP DOGG**
**and DAVID E. TALBERT**

"Look, I gotta go," she said, hanging up the phone.

This went on for the next few days. Sometimes I'd call and she'd answer and then hang up. At first I wondered how she knew it was me. Caller ID wasn't out yet—at least in Cali it wasn't. I even tried calling at different times, and still the same thing.

Not being able to stand it anymore, I made a rare appearance at high school, waiting for her after class.

"Ulysses, what the hell are you doing here? You scared the shit outta me," she said as I popped from around the corner.

"How else was I gonna see you?" I replied as she continued walking.

"You're not, that's how."

"Yo, what's going on?" I asked, blocking her from going any farther. "Is it somebody else?"

"No, it ain't nobody else."

"Then what is it?"

She paused, realizing that I wasn't going anywhere.

"They don't know you," she said, avoiding my eyes.

"Well then, why don't they get to know me?" I said, trying to force eye contact.

"It's not that easy," she said.

"It is if you let it be."

**Love Don't Live
Here No More**

She paused. I guess what she was saying without saying was that she was scared to bring me by the house. And regardless of how she felt about me, she knew her parents better than I did, so obviously she thought that they wouldn't approve.

"You scared to show me to your moms?" I asked.

"No, I ain't scared," she replied. "Not to show you to my mom at least, but my father . . . hell yeah, I'm scared."

"Scared about what?"

"You know what I'm scared about. You don't look like any of the boys I ever brought home."

"'Cause I *ain't* like any of the boys you ever brought home. I got home training," I said, finally getting her to look at me.

The bell rang for the beginning of the next class. Neither one of us moved, until finally, "Alright," Aisha said. "Tomorrow night. You come by the house at six o'clock. My father will just have gotten home. That's when you can meet him and my mother."

"Cool."

"Ulysses," she said, backing me against the hall locker, "don't come in smelling like that shit that you be smelling like."

**SNOOP DOGG and DAVID E. TALBERT**

"What you talking 'bout?"

"You know what I'm talking about. And put on some decent clothes. No sweatsuits, no tennis shoes. If you wanna meet my parents, you gotta meet 'em my way, not yours," she said, backing away and heading off to class. "And you better not have gotten me in trouble for being late," she continued, leaving me there alone in the hallway.

Shit. I didn't know what I had just gotten myself into. I guess like Mama always said, be careful what you pray for, 'cause you just might get it. And I just got it.

**Love Don't Live
Here No More**

# CHAPTER 18

# Rung the doorbell, went to hell

hat you worried about?" Herc said. "Just act like you usually act and everything'll be cool." He paused, looking at me. "On second thought, nigga, you in trouble," he said, laughing.

Herc had jokes, but at this point even his jokes couldn't make me laugh. This was about to be one of the hardest things ever. Probably because it was something I cared about. It was show and tell. In my mind, the worst thing that could possibly happen was about to. I was going to go over to Aisha's house and make a complete ass out of myself.

I could hardly sleep that night. Not because Uncle Mike was snoring, which he was, or because Bing was kicking me in the face with his stinky-ass feet, which he was, but because I was scared out of my mind about going to Aisha's house.

**Love Don't Live**
**Here No More**

I heard rattling through the door, and got up out of the bed to see what it was. It was Mama in the kitchen making herself some tea. She didn't get much alone time, so sometimes at night when she couldn't sleep, she'd make herself some tea and sit at the table to think.

"Hey, Mama," I said.

"What are you doing up? It's almost two o'clock in the morning."

"I couldn't sleep."

"Winkie is snoring again?" she asked.

"Yeah, but that's not it."

"Bing is kicking you in the face?"

"Yeah, but that's not it either."

"Then what is it?"

"What was Daddy like when he first met Grandma and Grandpa?"

"Now, why do you want to know that?" she asked.

"I don't know. Just curious," I said, taking a seat at the table.

"They hated him," she said, raising up and preparing her tea. "And for good reason, it turned out. The funny thing about parents is that they can see the end before the beginning."

**SNOOP DOGG**
**and DAVID E. TALBERT**

"Did you listen to 'em?"

"If I had, we wouldn't be here talking. Now would
we?"

"Right, right," I said.

"Why are you asking?" She picked up her cup and
began sipping her tea.

"No reason."

"Of course, there's a reason," she said, seeing right
through me. "You got a girlfriend?"

"Yeah."

"And you're gonna meet her parents."

"Yeah."

"And you're scared."

"Hell, yeah."

She knew me better than I knew myself.

"Ulysses, you ain't got nothing to be worried about,
just be yourself," she said, taking my hand in hers. "On
second thought . . . shit, you in trouble," she said, laughing. "Forgive me, Lord."

"You see that, Mama?" I said, snatching my hand
from hers. "You see that? That's jacked up."

I loved our relationship. Even with Harvey's bitch
ass, sorry-ass Uncle Mike, and Aunt Estelle Bible-
brainwashing her, every now and then it was just like

**Love Don't Live
Here No More**

old times and moments like this mattered when it was just her and me. She was still my best friend, and just laughing and talking with her made me realize how much I missed her.

"You remember this now, Ulysses. Anybody's parents who think you're not good enough for their daughter, their daughter ain't good enough for you," she said. "I don't care how big her ass is."

"Mama," I said, embarrassed. "How you know what I like?"

"'Cause I know what your daddy liked," she said, smiling. "Now give me a hug and take your ass to bed. Bing's toes are cold without having your forehead to keep 'em warm."

Moms was my girl. As usual, talking to her made me feel a lot better. Like most single moms, she had Bing and me at a young age, so it was almost like we grew up together, experiencing life, and dealing with change. Since it wasn't too long since she had been through it, she could relate to us going through it.

The next day arrived. It was the fastest day ever. Even Crazy Betty noticed I was acting strange.

"You're starting to act like my daughters," she said. "And I know why they act the way they act."

**SNOOP DOGG**
**and DAVID E. TALBERT**

All thoughts were leading to six o'clock. I paid her no mind.

As usual, I met Bing at the corner and we did our ghetto presto change-o.

We went back to the apartment, where I stood in front of the closet, flipping through my clothes, searching for just the right thing to wear.

"What you doin'?"

Of course, Bing was sitting up on the bed watching me.

"Don't worry about what I'm doing, man."

"Somebody needs to," he replied. "You've been staring into the closet for almost an hour."

Bing was more amused than worried, and watching me was probably more entertaining than anything that was on TV.

"Is there anything wrong with looking at the closet?" I said.

"No, but what you looking for?" he replied, walking over and standing right next to me.

"I'm having dinner tonight."

"With who, Aisha?" he asked.

"How do you know?"

"Uncle Mike don't snore that loud," he replied.

**Love Don't Live
Here No More**

"Well anyway, I'm looking for the right outfit. I got a dinner date with her mom and dad."

"You dating them, too?" he asked.

"No, dumb-ass. It's with her and her mom and her dad."

"Cool," he said. "How about these?"

He reached in my closet, pulling out a pair of blue slacks.

"And this," he continued, reaching for a button-down cream sweater that I'd gotten last Christmas but had never worn. Mama had the bad habit of buying me shit that she knew I didn't want to wear but that she hoped I would.

"And this," he said, handing me a short-sleeved white shirt. "And one more thing," he said, pulling out a red tie.

"You gon' make me look like an American flag," I said.

But he was probably right. Better safe than sorry. Looking like a suburban sissy was a small sacrifice. One that I didn't mind making for Aisha.

I quickly got dressed and walked down the hallway. Mama was waiting for me with a bittersweet smile on her face, like I was going off to war and she was never going to see me again.

"I'm so proud of you," she said. "You're becoming a man."

**SNOOP DOGG**
**and DAVID E. TALBERT**

"It's just dinner, Mama."

"That's what your father thought."

I reached Aisha's apartment building and buzzed the door.

Although we only lived three blocks apart, it was like a whole different world. It was still the 'hood, but just the happier 'hood.

On her block, the homeless people had blankets. The buzzer worked on the apartment door, and you didn't have to step over ten people to reach it.

*Bzzzz.*

Almost immediately, the door unlocked. There was no turning back now.

She lived in apartment 406. I tapped.

"I got it, Mama!" Aisha's voice rang out.

"No, *I* got it."

Aw, shit. I was sure she was going to dress me up and down, telling me some shit like "Aisha's not at home," or "She don't date dudes like you," or "How come you ain't become a candidate for baptism at the church." Whatever negative thought I could think of, I was thinking. Just as I was ready to turn to walk away, I heard the sound of three or four chains sliding open from inside. The door quickly opened and there she

**Love Don't Live
Here No More**

was. Aisha's mom, looking almost finer than her daughter. She was a beautiful brown-skinned woman, with hair down to her shoulders, probably her own, and full breasts, probably her own. They didn't have fake titties in the 'hood. At least not back then. Back in the day, she was probably knocking them dead herself, and they were knocking her dead too, no doubt.

Looking at her let me know what I'd be looking at twenty years from now with Aisha, and if it was, I wouldn't be mad. She was trump tight. I could see why her father stayed around. Shit, I would, too.

"Can I help you?" she said, smiling.

"Yeah. I mean, yes, ma'am. I'm Ulysses."

"Ulysses?" she asked, looking at me curiously.

"I'm Aisha's boy . . . uh . . . her friend," I said, looking like one of Crazy Betty's kids.

"*Ohhhh*. Ulysses. The one she met at church. Yes. Come right in," she said, welcoming me into her home.

Damn, they were living good. I guess you could live like this when your father's around, or at least when your uncle and play father weren't. They had couches and loveseats, end tables—wasn't a piece of plastic in sight. On the walls hung black art like you saw on *Good Times*. Their house even smelled better. Not like the chicken grease and fish oil I was used to. Theirs smelled like air freshener.

"Melissa, who's that at the door?" boomed a voice from the back.

"It's Aisha's boy . . ." Her mom paused, smiling at me. "Her friend."

Seconds later, he walked through the door looking relaxed, his shirt out of his pants, brown slippers on his feet. Her father was about six feet tall. He looked solid, like he was in the military, sporting a regulation haircut and round wire-rimmed glasses.

He walked over to me and extended his hand. I gave him mine. From his grip alone, I knew, if need be, an ass-whipping was not out of the realm of possibilities.

"How you doin', son?" he said.

"I'm fine, sir. You got a nice house. It smells good."

He shot me a strange look, releasing my hand.

"Aisha!"

I heard a door crack.

Given the fact that I hadn't seen her yet, she was obviously more nervous than I was, staying as far away from the initial introduction as she could.

"You have company out here," he continued.

"I'll be right out," she said.

**Love Don't Live Here No More**

"So, where'd you two meet? School?"

"Nah. I mean, no, sir."

"They met at church," her mother said.

"*Ohhhh.* Church, yes. Your mother and father attend there?"

"Hell na . . . I mean, no, sir," I said. "My mother does and my brother and I, and, well, she's got a friend and he goes sometimes, when he feels like it."

"A friend?" he said.

Her mother cleared her throat, giving Aisha's father a sign to let it go.

Shortly after, Aisha came out, breaking the awkward moment.

"So, Aisha," her father said. "You two are friends?"

"Yes, sir," she said.

"How good of friends?" he asked, raising his eyebrow, giving me *the look.*

I had dated enough girls to know what *the look* meant. It usually didn't come from their father because he was never around. It usually came from their mother or big brother or uncle.

"Henry," the mother chimed in. "You're embarrassing him."

"We're pretty good friends, Daddy," Aisha said.

**SNOOP DOGG**
**and DAVID E. TALBERT**

"I guess so. You stay up talking on the phone all hours of the night," he continued. "Does your mama know you're on the phone like that, son?"

"Yes, sir."

"Does her *friend* know, too?"

"Henry! That is none of your business."

"It's alright, Mrs. Parker," I said, turning to Aisha's father. "To be honest, sir, I don't really know," I said, pausing. "But if he did, it really wouldn't matter, seeing as my mother's paying all the bills and he's just creating more."

Aisha's eyes widened. Her mother's followed. The next thing I expected was to be thrown out of the house by my collar, never seeing or hearing from Aisha again. Then unexpectedly her father laughed.

It started off small, then grew louder. Soon after, Aisha's mother laughed, too. Then Aisha joined in. Shit, since they were laughing, I figured I might as well join in, too. We were all laughing.

"Son, I think I like you," he said. "Well, the game's on in the back, so I'ma get back to watching it. It was a pleasure meeting you," he said, extending his hand, this time keeping it firmly gripped in mine. "I like you," he said as his laughter trailed off, "but I'll kill you. Do we understand each other?"

**Love Don't Live
Here No More**

I nodded.

He released my hand and walked away.

"Will you be joining us for dinner?" Aisha's mother asked.

"Sure, if that's not a problem," I replied.

"I think you passed the test. So it's no problem at all," she said, smiling, walking toward her kitchen.

Aisha smiled. I smiled.

And for a moment at least, it was all good in the Long Beach 'hood.

**SNOOP DOGG**
**and DAVID E. TALBERT**

# CHAPTER

# 19

Life is
a lesson/
'cause life is
so vicious

Now I could call Aisha any-
time I wanted to.

Most of the times
when I called, her mom would want to talk to me longer than Aisha would, and when I came over, she'd
pull me into the kitchen to sample whatever she
was cooking. She was excited to have someone new
around to appreciate her food. I guess if you eat a
person's cooking long enough, no matter how good
it is, you become spoiled and stop appreciating the
effort that was put in. Now, she couldn't cook better than my mama. Nobody could. But I'm not one to
turn down a meal, especially a good one, whether my
mama cooked it or not.

Sometimes even her father picked up the phone just
to say hello, talk about sports, or sometimes even about
the sermon on Sunday, which of course since I was
asleep, I really didn't know what the hell he was talk-

**Love Don't Live
Here No More**

ing about. But since most of my conversations with him were spent listening more than talking to him, it really didn't matter.

I was in.

It probably had something to do with the fact that Aisha and I met at church. They had no idea that me and my brother had to be damn near forced at gunpoint to attend, but however it came, it was a blessing nonetheless. I guess I owed God one for this.

Things were going well. Aisha and I hadn't had sex yet, but we had done just about everything else.

"Yo, man, you gon' hang out with your girl or you gon' make music?" Herc said. "You can't do both."

"Why you salty?" I asked.

"'Bout what? I got bitches, too, you know. The difference is I don't let my bitches run me."

"Yeah, okay, Herc."

"Yeah, okay, my ass. Don't sleep," Herc said. "I got bitches. Just 'cause you don't see 'em don't mean they ain't here. Anyway, I got a hookup to get us into this party. Yo, you down?"

"Of course I'm down."

"It's a freestyle party. You know, niggas in the 'hood who can't rap bumrush the mic and act like they can.

Like you," he said, laughing, "before you started fucking with me."

"You mean before you started fucking with *me*."

"Whatever," Herc said. "Anyway, I figured we make it our coming-out party. Let 'em know we for real. I mean, you know, if that's alright with your girl."

"Okay, so you got jokes."

"Nah, I'm just sayin'. We can't write rhymes forever. At some point we gotta perform 'em. You know, manifest destiny."

"What the *hell* are you talking about?"

"I'm talking 'bout our founding fathers. In the mid-1800s, they felt they had the divine right to expand and take over this country. They was like, 'Fuck the Indians. This our shit, and we gon' take it. By any means necessary.'"

"Where do you get this shit?" I asked.

"School, muthafucka. You know, the place you ain't been for four months? Rhyming is *our* manifest destiny. It's divine."

As crazy as that shit sounded, it was the truth. Between Aisha, Buddha, and keeping a handle on the homefront, I had lost my passion. Like Buddha said, "You always gotta have another hustle. And whatever that hustle is, it's gotta be something you love."

**Love Don't Live
Here No More**

Rhyming was my love. My destiny. My manifest destiny.

Herc took off and I followed behind him.

"What year was that shit again?" I asked.

"*Encyclopaedia Britannica*, dumb fuck. Pick it up. You might learn something."

We both laughed as we headed home to work on some beats.

# CHAPTER

20

# See if you
## feel my pain . . .
### one more game

The freestyle party was my time to shine.

Cats were supposed to be coming off the dome, but I heard more rehearsed and rehashed elementary school rhymes than anything.

Knocking these cats out the box was all I was thinking about.

"I thought you was taking me out to the movies tonight?" Aisha said, with an attitude that let me know she wasn't too happy with the change of plans.

"I was, but I can't."

"Why can't you?"

"'Cause I can't."

"Why?"

"'Cause I'm rollin' with Herc," I said, not wanting to tell her the real reason.

"Herc, huh?" she said.

"Yeah, Herc."

**Love Don't Live Here No More**

"Well, I hope you two have a good time," she said, slipping her hand on my thigh and moving it slowly upward, downward, and upward again.

"Girl, what you doin'?" I said. My temperature wasn't the only thing rising.

"What it feel like I'm doin'?" she said, cupping me, squeezing my jimmy. "You know what? You go ahead with your boy Herc tonight. 'Cause I'm sure," she said, kissing me once on the lips, "Herc can do this for you, too."

"If he could, I wouldn't let him," I said.

"I hope not," she said, sticking her tongue down my throat. "I'm not trippin', though. I could see why you would want to hang out with Herc," she said, kissing my spot, "and not me. I mean, if it were me, I'd rather hang out with a dude than hang out with something soft," she said, kissing me on my ear, "wet"—she licked her tongue down the back of my neck—"and warm."

She stood back as I was damn near in a daze.

"Have fun," she said, walking away, breaking every stitch in her jeans, switching that ass, leaving me there thinking, *If this party ain't good, I'm whipping Herc's ass.*

"I'ma call you, Aisha," I said.

"Whatever," she said, not turning around.

"And you better not pick up and hang up."

**SNOOP DOGG**
**and DAVID E. TALBERT**

"Whatever," she said, this time with more attitude.

We got to the party and Herc's hookup wasn't really a hookup. The door opened and slammed almost at the same time.

"I thought you said we could get in?" I said, fuming. "I oughta whip your ass."

"'Cause we can't get in? To a party?" he replied.

"Cuz, you don't know what I gave up for this."

"Relax. Shit," he said as the windows shook from the loud music that was playing inside. It was Deshon's party, our friend Chauncey's cousin. His cousin Peron threw parties at the club and Deshon threw them at the house. I guess promoting and partying kind of ran in their family.

"Yo, man, I'ma get you in," Chauncey said, sticking his head out the door. "Just gimme a few minutes."

"We already gave you a few minutes," I said, as fine-ass women were walking in and out of the house, looking at us wondering why we weren't doing the same. "I oughta whip your ass, Chauncey."

He and Herc both looked at me as Chauncey went back in the house.

"Nigga, what is wrong with you?" Herc asked. "Why you trying to fight everybody?"

**Love Don't Live Here No More**

"'Cause I coulda been with Aisha, that's why," I said. "Instead, we lookin' like busters, the only fools standing outside waiting to get into a house party."

"*Ohhhh*. I shoulda known," Herc said. "Question. How you get pussywhipped before you get the pussy? How does that happen? Explain that to me. Do you wanna rap or do you wanna romance? You gotta make up your mind, 'cause you can't have both."

"Maybe I wanna rap about romance, did you ever think about that?"

"What the hell is that?" Herc said.

"I'm going home, that's what the fuck it is."

Just as we were about to break into one of our usual arguments, we heard Chauncey whispering from the side of the house.

"Yo, yo, man, come on! We gon' slip through the back."

"The back? Why can't we go in through the front?"

"Will you shut the fuck up," Herc said. "We gettin' in. For free."

We followed him, damn near cutting half our arms off on the thorns in the bushes.

"Damn!" I shouted.

"Oh man, I forgot to tell you," Chauncey said. "They got rosebushes."

At this point, whether the party was good or not, I was still whipping Herc's ass. And maybe even Chauncey's.

"Oh yeah, and watch the steps," Chauncey added. "The concrete's all fucked up."

It was too late. We had already nearly broken our necks on the back porch steps where the concrete was crumbling apart.

I shot Herc a look.

We were finally inside. The party was just as off the hook as we'd imagined.

It was wall-to-wall niggas. And bitches, too.

"See, I told you. You gon' listen to me one day," Herc said, pulling the last thorn from his arm.

He was right, though I'd never admit it to him. Writing rhymes was one thing, but rocking the crowd was another. It didn't matter how many nights we practiced, me on the mic that Buddha had bought and Herc scratching on his mama's worn-out record player hooked up to the sampler. Nothing would compare to the real deal: Herc on the ones and twos and me on the mic turning the party out.

Cats were already freestyling.

"They ain't even that good," Herc said. "I told you, man . . . that's us."

Herc was the Flavor Flav of Long Beach. The hype

**Love Don't Live**
**Here No More**

man. A ghetto Svengali. If I didn't already believe I was good, listening to Herc long enough made me think I was the G.O.A.T.

It was cats from all over. Rollin' 60 Crips from South Central, 20s from Long Beach, Pirus from Compton, and Grape Street was representing Watts. Even posers from the Valley came dressed in red *and* blue, not really knowing which one they wanted to be or why. I'm sure they would have gotten a beatdown, but cats knew they were from the Valley, so they gave 'em a pass.

"Them fools on the mic ain't half as good as you," Herc said. "Not half. I'm telling you, man, that should be you, that should be me. They can't touch us. Yo, I'ma get us on," Herc said as he weaved his way through the crowd.

"Hold up!" I called after him, being bumped by two or three penitentiary-sized cats. I lost him in the throng of people. Knowing Herc, the next time I would hear from him again was when he was introducing me to the crowd.

"Yo, Herc!" I shouted again, to no avail.

Suddenly there was a tap on my shoulder. I turned around.

Aw, shit. It was Mishi. She had more cakes than Duncan Hines. Looking thicker than a Snickers, but with more drama than the soaps.

**SNOOP DOGG**
**and DAVID E. TALBERT**

"Where you been?" she said, popping her gum, gliding her tongue over her top four teeth.

"I been where I always been, handling mines," I said.

"I know you been doing your thing," she said, twirling her dookie braids. "But who you been doing it with?"

She came closer, pressing her chest against mine.

Mishi and I had been off and on, on and back off, and then just off. I wouldn't be surprised if she wasn't a virgin when we met. I mean, I know women develop faster than men, but damn. At fourteen, she was doing shit that chicks who were eighteen didn't know about. She was like a child prodigy. A little Bobby Fischer, sexually speaking. Either that or a hoe.

"What's up, Mishi?" random cats would shout as we were walking.

"How come you don't call a nigga!" another guy would shout as he drove by.

She would act like they were just clowning, but in my mind they had been swimming . . . in her.

She had me turned out before I knew what "turned out" was. So the first few times this happened, it really didn't matter. But by the thirtieth and fortieth time, I'd had enough.

**Love Don't Live
Here No More**

"I was saving myself for you," she would always say. "You're the only one."

Though she would never admit it, in my heart I knew I was "the only one" of many.

"You got my number, right?" she said.

"Yeah, I got it," I replied, her thigh now pressed against mine.

"Well, use it, then," she said.

"Maybe I will."

"In a minute," she said, walking away, leaving me there frozen in thought, rewinding our relationship. The good times. The even more bad times. And the even more good sex.

"That skeezer still got you open," Herc said. "Well, maybe this'll help—she's fucking Chauncey's cousin, Peron. Are you over it now?"

I couldn't do nothing but shake my head. Herc had just derailed my trip down memory lane.

"Now come on," he said again, making his way through the crowd.

This time I followed. Elbow to elbow, shoulder to shoulder, right behind him.

"Where we goin'?" I asked.

"You'll find out when we get there," he said.

**SNOOP DOGG**
**and DAVID E. TALBERT**

"Get where?"

"To the eye of the storm, the belly of the beast, the center of the universe. Man, you up next."

"You mean, we up next," I said.

"Nah, *you* up next. I'ma be on the turntables. They only got one mic and it's got your name on it."

We were on one side of the room, waiting for what seemed like forever. The cats on the mic were wack. Couldn't rhyme their way out of a Dr. Seuss book. They had damn near emptied out the party. Fools were cussin'. One even hurled an empty bottle of Olde E. that went crashing upside dude's head, but that still wasn't enough to make him give up the mic. Some cats just didn't get it. You'd think a bottle on the forehead would help them get the message.

With a microphone in your hand, you were like a god, and no matter how rough it got or how awful you were, it was a power many weren't quick to give up.

It was like a bad episode of *Showtime at the Apollo*. The only things missing were Sandman, a broom, and a siren.

In mid-rhyme, a hand grabbed the mic and another snatched the rapper by the collar. It was Chauncey's cousin Deshon and one of his boys, who'd realized that if dude went on any longer, the party would be over.

**Love Don't Live Here No More**

Seconds later, two more hands snatched the deejay along with him. He wasn't rapping, but he was just as guilty.

It didn't take a rocket scientist to know what to do next. Herc hit the tables. I grabbed the mic. And with barely a pause in the music, the party was back on track.

Herc threw on The Ohio Players. "Skin Tight." The crowd went wild.

He had the cross-faders screaming, mixing his ass off. So much so, I forgot what I was supposed to be doing and was in awe watching him. He cradled the headphones in the crook of his neck.

"You gon' watch me," he said, "or they gon' watch you?"

That was my cue.

It was what I had been rehearsing for all my life. All I had was the mic, a shot, and a dream. My moment of truth. And with the mic firmly gripped in my hand, I shot a look to Herc and he shot one back, knowing we were about to own it.

And that's just what we did.

We were no longer just talking about it.

We were being about it.

**SNOOP DOGG**
**and DAVID E. TALBERT**

# CHAPTER

# 21

Should **you**
**stay/** or just
**walk** away

next Friday was the same. And the Friday after that. Crashing one party after the other, not spending nearly the kind of time with Aisha that I used to.

"You going to a party *again*?" she said.

She really wasn't feeling me or my commitment to realizing my dream. It was like we were back where we had started. I would call, she would pick up and then hang up. It was happening so many times that I'm sure her mother was doing it, too.

I had chosen rapping over romance, spending more time with the mic than with my main piece. Rapping had finally become real to me. Getting the chance to do what cats like G-Bang were doing was the main thing we were focused on.

"If I could just get you to start selling as much you love rhyming, we'd all be millionaires," Buddha said, joking.

**Love Don't Live
Here No More**

I could tell he was proud, but at the same time he was reminding me of the business at hand.

Even things between Mama and Harvey seemed better. Not that they were, but I wasn't around enough for it to matter as much. By the time I made it home from rehearsing with Herc, not even Uncle Mike's snores could keep me up, nor the occasional kick in the chin from Bing's right foot.

We were hopping from one party to another, rocking the mic. Because Chauncey had the hookup, he took us all around Long Beach, and sometimes even L.A. One time he took us to the Valley to a party full of white folks, Asians, and black folks who acted like white folks and Asians. Instead of forties and chicken wings, they were serving sushi and lite beer. We still rocked it.

"You going out *again*?" Bing said.

If he was old enough, I would have brought him with me. But the last thing I needed was more eyes on me than there already were.

One time I called Aisha and got her to pick up, but as soon as she heard my voice, *click!*

Not able to stand it anymore, there I was back in school, hanging out in the hallway waiting for her to leave class.

"*Aisha!*" I called.

**SNOOP DOGG
and DAVID E. TALBERT**

She kept walking. I rushed after her, cutting her off.

"What?" she said, giving me the look that women give when they really ain't feeling you.

"How come you be hanging up on me all the time?"

"You know why," she said.

"'Cause I'm doin' what I love?"

"'Cause you ain't doin' who you love. Or at least who you claim to."

The bell rang.

"Just call me later," she said, walking to her class.

"If I do, you gon' hang up?"

"Probably," she said, not turning around.

"Then why you want me to call?"

She didn't answer.

"Aisha!"

"She's just trippin'," Herc said. "If she didn't, how else would you know she was a woman? Yo, Chauncey got the hookup on this party off Crenshaw and King. It's Chauncey's third cousin, Max."

How many cats in this family threw parties?

This time when we got there, we didn't have any problem getting in. We were 'hood famous. Everybody knew that if we were at a party, it was shonuf gonna get rocked.

**Love Don't Live
Here No More**

"See, what'd I tell you," Herc said. "We known."

It wasn't really a freestyle party, but since they had a deejay and a microphone, it was a perfect place for us to crash. I started spitting on the mic, Herc behind me, mixing and scratching. We had the party on hit. They had even started shouting my name.

I gave Herc a look. He shot it back. Then his eyes shifted to the front door, and a look of worry covered his face. It was Chino and three of his boys.

This was why I didn't like going into L.A. I was out of my element with no protection.

I stopped rhyming, then started backing up as Chino and I made eye contact. He lifted his right hand and pointed at me as if it were a gun, pulling the trigger with his index finger.

We watched Chino and his boys making their way through the crowd, dapping, nodding, getting recognized by damn near everybody in the spot.

We were smack in the middle of enemy territory.

Herc and I signaled to each other, both knowing it was time to bounce.

With the record still spinning, Herc with a handful of vinyl and me with the mic Buddha gave me clutched tightly in my hand, we jetted toward the back door.

**SNOOP DOGG**
**and DAVID E. TALBERT**

"Yo, watch yourself, cuz!"

"Yo, can I have my foot back!"

Various people shouted at us as we weaved our way through the crowd, hoping to get lost.

A familiar voice cut through the noise.

"What I gotta do to get on your menu?"

It was Aisha, blocking my path.

"What the hell are you doing here?"

"To see you," she said. "I wanted to surprise you."

"Yo, come on, man," Herc said. "We gotta get outta here."

I grabbed Aisha by the arm.

"What are you doing?" she shouted over the music.

"Just come on," I said as I pulled her along.

We had just about made it to the back door when one of Chino's boys stepped in our way.

We turned to the left. There was another.

Then right. Another.

We turned around.

There stood Chino.

"*Oye, mira,* how you gon' get the party started and leave?" he said. "I was just starting to enjoy myself," he continued, motioning to his boys. "Why would you wanna leave all the sexy *muchachas*? Oh, I see why," he said,

**Love Don't Live
Here No More**

looking at Aisha. "You brought your own *mija, muy bonita. Yo quiero coger a tu chica en el culo.*"

His boys laughed as he slipped his hand under his jacket between his waist and his buckle.

"Yo, fuck you!" Aisha said.

"My pleasure, *mija.*" Chino smiled, turning to me. "Do you mind?"

Buddha was right. This muthafucka was out of control.

"Fuck you," I said.

"Everybody wants to fuck me," he said, turning to his boys. They laughed. "So you rappin' now, holmes?" he said, as I felt one of his boys shove me with his forearm in the small of my back.

I didn't respond.

"You was all up on the microphone and shit. Your *putita* over there spinnin' on the turntables."

"I got your bitch, bitch," Herc said as two of Chino's boys stepped closer.

Chino laughed, giving his boys the eye to let that go. "Where's Buddha? The *vato*'s hearing footsteps," he said, as his boys chuckled. "Give him a message for me, Tone Loc. I'm knocking. You tell him I said that. *Comprende?*"

**SNOOP DOGG**
**and DAVID E. TALBERT**

Chino stared me down, then turned to Aisha, raping her with his eyes. Then to Herc.

"As for you having my bitch," he said, his three boys closing in on us, "*tu madre* was *mi puta anoche.*"

Whatever the hell he was saying, the shit had to be foul. I couldn't just let him punk us, diss my girl, and get away with bad-mouthing Buddha. Just as I was about to crack this fool in the head with my mic, fate intervened.

"Y'all break that shit up."

It was Chauncey's cousin, Max. Standing beside him were five more cats, bigger than Chino's.

"You need to slow your roll, 'cause you fuck with my cousin's friends, you fucking with me and my boys," he continued, eyeing Chino and his three dudes.

Chino paused, then smiled.

"We were just wondering why the entertainment was leaving," he said to Max. He nodded at his boys, and then walked away, his one boy shoving me again in the back just to let me know that this shit had ended prematurely.

I was glad that Max and his boys were there, 'cause we would have got our asses whipped. I might have gotten the first lick in, but it would have damn sure been my last.

**Love Don't Live
Here No More**

Herc, Aisha, and I left out the back door. It was a good thing Herc had borrowed his mother's car, because this was not the time to be walking, whether it was our neighborhood or not. Neither one of us were saying much of anything, just watching the rear- and sideview mirrors, making sure nobody rolled up on us.

"We rocked that shit, though, didn't we?" Herc said, breaking the silence.

"Yeah, a hollow point almost rocked us," I replied.

Aisha sat in the back with her arms folded, staring out the window.

"Better to live for something than die for nothing," he said.

"What the fuck are you talking about?" Aisha said.

Herc looked at me.

"Is she talking to you, 'cause I know she ain't talking to me," he said.

"I'm talking to both of y'all. We coulda got killed to-night, and y'all sitting up in here making jokes. And why the hell am I sitting in the back?"

"I'm sure it ain't the first backseat you've seen."

"Fuck you," Aisha replied.

"Hey, hey, man," I said to Herc. "Chill out."

**SNOOP DOGG**
**and DAVID E. TALBERT**

"Me? You need to say that to your girl, 'cause last I remember, she wasn't even invited. I coulda made her ass walk home."

"Let me out, then."

The car screeched to a halt.

"Tuck and roll," Herc said. "Tuck and muthafuckin' roll."

The back door opened. Aisha got out and stomped off down Stocker, past the Liquor Bank.

"Did you have to do that, man?" I asked.

"Yes. 'Cause if you won't check her, guess what? I will."

I swung the door open.

"Don't leave," I said, looking back at Herc.

I ran after Aisha, who had damn near speedwalked her way up the hill to Valley Ridge.

"Isha! Hold up!"

I ran to catch up with her. Herc's car creeped slowly behind.

"What are you doing?" I said, out of breath. "Get back in the car."

She kept walking.

"Aisha," I said, grabbing her arm. She snatched it away. "What is wrong with you?"

**Love Don't Live Here No More**

"No, what is wrong with *you*?" she snapped, finally stopping and turning on me.

"Let's leave her ass," Herc shouted. "I gotta have my mama's car home by midnight."

"Shut the fuck up, Herc," I said. "Aisha. Talk to me."

"Do you care about me?" she asked.

"You know I care about you."

"Do you care about yourself? 'Cause if you don't care about yourself, you can't possibly care about me."

I paused, not knowing what to say.

"I can't do this, Ulysses."

"Can't do what?"

"This. You. Us. I really like you, Ulysses. But I don't live like this. I can't live like this."

"Aisha, what are you talking about?"

"You're a drug dealer. That's what I'm talking about."

"You knew what I was when you met me. You didn't have a problem with it before when I was taking you to the movies and out to eat and buying you shit. Now it's a problem."

"I love you, Ulysses. That's the problem."

Her words hung in the air. Besides my mama and my

grandmama, no woman had ever told me she loved me, and meant it.

"What do you want from me?" I asked after a moment.

"I want you to make a choice, Ulysses."

I just stared at her.

"Can we choose to take our asses back to Long Beach before we become victims of a drive-by?" Herc said.

Aisha's eyes were locked on mine.

"Come on," I said. "Let's go."

She gently shook her head and walked over to the car. She opened the back door and got in.

We jumped on the 405 and headed home. Nobody said a word the entire way.

We dropped Aisha off first. Before Herc could bring the car to a full stop, she had hopped out the back and rushed inside.

"What an ungrateful bitch," Herc said, shaking his head. "She didn't even say thank you. You're welcome!" he shouted through the window.

The security gate slammed and she was gone.

"You hungry?" Herc asked. "My mama got some leftover meat loaf. We can make some sandwiches."

**Love Don't Live
Here No More**

"Nah, man. Just drop me at the house."

Moments later, we pulled up in front of my apartment.

"We did rock that shit," Herc said.

He pounded me up, and then pulled off.

I walked to my apartment building thinking I'd never felt so full and empty at the same time.

**SNOOP DOGG**
**and DAVID E. TALBERT**

# CHAPTER

# 22

# It's lonely outside/ if only I tried

It was just past midnight. I opened the bedroom door and there was Bing sitting up alone, staring out the window.

"Yo, what's up, man?" I said.

"What's up?"

"Where's Mike?" I asked.

"He left out," Bing said.

"What's wrong with you?"

"Nothing."

"Bing," I said, grabbing his arm and turning him around, "what's wrong?"

"Mama."

"What about her?"

"She lost her job again."

I rushed out of the room and knocked softly on her door. No one answered. I knocked a little harder. Still

**Love Don't Live
Here No More**

no answer. Just as I was about to bang on it, the door opened.

"What's up?" Harvey asked, looking wide-awake and ashy in a wifebeater and some boxer shorts. "It's not a good time right now."

"Nigga, get out the way," I said, trying to step around him.

He stepped in front of me.

"I said, it's not a good time right now," Harvey repeated. "Lots going on."

"Man, if you don't get out of my way," I said.

"I'll talk to you in the morning, Ulysses," I heard Mama say, sounding as if all the life had been sucked out of her.

"But, Mama, I—"

"Good night, Ulysses," she said.

"One of these days you gon' listen," Harvey smirked, and closed the door.

Seconds later the front door opened. It was Uncle Mike.

"Nephew," he said, his breath smelling like cheap liquor, "can I talk to you for a minute?"

"Ulysses. The name is Ulysses."

I turned my face and walked toward the bedroom,

not wanting to hear or smell what was coming out of his
mouth.

"Ulysses!" he said, stopping me in my tracks. "We
need to talk."

He turned around, headed toward the front door,
opened it, and waited for me to follow.

"Please," he said.

Everything about this night was strange. I followed
him. We stepped outside and stood in the hallway, closing the door behind us.

"Look here, nephew." He paused. "Ulysses. No matter what you may think about me, I love your mama," he
said. I could barely hear him over the TV blaring out of
the apartment next door. "Your mama just lost her job.
But I'm sure you already know that. She got a lot on
her."

"You think?" I said. "She got two grown-ass men who
ain't bringing shit to the table but an appetite."

"I deserve that, and maybe Harvey does, too," he
said with an unusual look of sincerity. "But your mama,
she don't. Look here, nephew," he said, stepping closer,
whispering, "I know what you're doing."

"What you mean, you know what I'm—"

"I know, 'cause I used to do it, too. You ain't foolin'

**Love Don't Live
Here No More**

nobody, and you damn sure ain't foolin' me, leaving out the front door, coming through the back. These walls got ears and the streets got eyes." He paused, looking at me. "I know you got money. You got it, and your mama needs it. Now you and me know she ain't gon' take it from you. But she'll take it from me," he said.

I listened closely.

"So look here, nephew. What you gon' do is take some of that money you make, give it to me, and I'll give it to her. She ain't gotta know where it's coming from, that ain't important. What's important is who it's going to."

"How do I know I can trust you?" I asked, thinking that the smell of cheap liquor on his breath would soon be replaced by the smell of something much more expensive.

"'Cause before she was your mama, she was my sister. And before I used to have to listen to your shit, I used to clean it. And the only reason I haven't slapped the taste out of your mouth every time you disrespected me is because I know you're too young and ignorant to know any better. And more important, because I know you love your mama. You may hate me 'cause I ain't shit, but don't let your hate for me block your love for her."

For a moment, I forgot about how sick to my stomach he made me. The times he had burdened my mother, making his problems hers. I reached in my pocket and handed him five hundred dollars.

"You make sure she gets this," I said.

He placed the money in his pocket.

He went to hug me and caught himself as we both realized that, even in times like these, it still wasn't that kind of relationship. He headed back inside the apartment as I stood outside the door, pondering. The last thing in the world I wanted to see was my mother going through it, especially when I knew I could help. He was right. She would never take any money from me. I wouldn't either.

Mama was poor, but she was proud. Taking money from a son that was dealing drugs would have been like taking a bullet in her heart. It would have been a sign that she had failed in giving her sons the better lives she had hoped we'd have.

For the next few weeks, I continued giving Uncle Mike money. I guess she never asked questions about where it was coming from. She knew he wasn't working, but I guess a question never asked is a question never answered. Five hundred here when he said she was short

**Love Don't Live
Here No More**

on the rent. Three hundred there when he said the carburetor went out her car. Whatever I could give, I would.

I was finally contributing to the household in a way I had always imagined I would, even if I did have to go through Uncle Mike to do it. Mama was the glue that held our family together, and without it, things would quickly unravel.

This continued for weeks, and still Mama couldn't find a job.

Uncle Mike started hitting me up for more money more often.

"Yo, nephew, it's the first of the month. You know she ain't got it."

Again five hundred dollars.

"Yo, nephew, you seen any groceries in the refrigerator lately?"

Another hundred dollars.

Seventy-five more for the lights. A hundred and fifty more for the water bill from Harvey's ass taking thirty-five-minute showers. I was the ATM of the LBC, shooting out cash daily.

How could I say no?

Until one day I didn't have to.

I came home and Uncle Mike was gone. Bing was,

too. Lying on the bed that used to be mine was an eviction notice.

That muthafucka hadn't been giving my mother shit.

I picked up the notice and stuffed it in my bag, planning to take care of it myself. I knocked on Mama's bedroom door. She wasn't home, either. Just Harvey.

"She ain't here," he barked.

It wasn't even an option that I might want to talk to him.

Something more than just not having money was wrong.

Whatever it was, I was about to find out.

**Love Don't Live
Here No More**

# CHAPTER 23

I'm a
**dough boy/**
and **no** I ain't
givin' it **up**

**T**his was beginning to happen more times than not.

Mama and Bing always seemed to be gone and only Harvey was there, looking half asleep or drunk—I couldn't tell the difference. And I really didn't care.

Aunt Estelle was even dropping by more times than usual.

"The Lord works in mysterious ways," she said. "And sometimes the ways ain't that mysterious. You just have to open your eyes and see 'em. Adam would have never ate the apple if he had just opened his eyes," she continued. "You remember what I'm saying, you hear me? You remember what I'm saying."

Even she was acting strange. More strange than normal, talking in riddles. Everybody in the house knew something but me. I was asking, but nobody was talking.

**Love Don't Live Here No More**

It had been weeks and still no sign of Uncle Mike. It was probably best for all parties involved because the next time I saw him was going to be the last time anybody saw him. I could halfway forgive him if it was me. But taking from Mama and Bing was beyond shiesty.

Family could be real fucked up.

Mama said she had found a part-time job, but Herc borrowed his mother's car again and we followed her one day. She drove five blocks, turned the corner, pulled up on a side street, and sat there for hours. Then she turned around and came back home. This happened more than a few times.

Like I said, she was proud.

"Ain't no free meal," she would always say. The last thing Mama would want was for me and Bing to see her just sitting around waiting. Watching Uncle Mike doing that for the last couple of months was bad enough.

I wanted to help her out so bad, I paid the rent that month. But when she found out, she was furious.

"I don't know where you got this money from, Ulysses. But wherever you got it, take it right back."

She finally found a job cleaning houses. She would come home reeking of ammonia. I could see this was killing her. Though she only had a high school education, she was still smarter than anyone I'd ever known, accustomed to using her head more than her hands.

"Mama, I can help."

She would ignore me, walking in real late and leaving out real early.

Even when she wasn't working, she and Bing were out of the house more than usual. And still nobody was talking.

Outside of the house wasn't any better.

Crazy Betty was temporarily shut down. One of her daughters accidentally burned her hand on the stove. The state put Crazy Betty on probation, claiming she was unfit. Maybe she was high and hadn't been paying attention. Maybe that was just the kind of shit that happened when you had special kids with special needs. Either way, her being shut down meant I was being shut down.

"A burnt hand ain't a burnt house," Crazy Betty said. "Just 'cause they threw out the baby, we still got the bathwater."

She handed me a set of keys to her old rusted brown Buick LeSabre that she kept parked across the street. My shop was temporarily relocated. It was the perfect spot. Even though it didn't have tint, enough dirt had piled up on the windows from the car never moving that

**Love Don't Live Here No More**

it was just as good, if not better. Nobody could see in and the only way I could see out was by cracking the window when I heard the designated code. Two taps on the front hubcap on the passenger side. The money came in and product went out.

The shit was getting crazy.

It seemed like the walk from the apartment to the car was getting harder and harder every day. Dodging Mama, sneaking by Bing, ignoring Harvey. Then occasionally being questioned by cops that rolled past from time to time.

"Ain't this a school day?" one would ask. "You ain't gon' never make it to college skipping school," he said laughing, pulling off. Laughing because he knew that college was the last place anybody from around here was going.

I was a mark. If the customers could reach me so easily, then so could anybody else, which was not a good thing. Especially since the beef between Buddha and Chino had spiraled out of control.

Cats that were around one day were gone the next. One day, one of Buddha's. The next day, two of Chino's. Bullets were raining from one side of Long Beach to the other. There was so much gunfire that you were surprised when things got quiet. The symphony of sirens filled the air both day and night.

"You need to take these, YG," Buddha said, handing me two Glock 9s. "If you man enough to pull it out, be man enough to use it," he said as I put one in my bag and cradled the other in my hand.

The shit had gone to a whole 'nother level. Buddha even had one of his boys making regular checks on the corner near my house.

"I don't take shit for granted," Buddha said. "Niggas that fuck with you will fuck with your family."

For the next few days, I even told Bing to act like he was sick just to keep him off the street and in the house.

I left out early, posting in Crazy Betty's car across the street, making sure Mama got out of the apartment and in her car safely and back again. I didn't say shit to Harvey. I was halfway hoping there was a stray bullet out there with his name on it.

"How long I gotta be sick?" Bing asked.

"Until I tell you to get better," I replied.

"Cool!" he said.

For him it was like summer vacation, only in the winter.

**Love Don't Live
Here No More**

That night Mama came home late with a strange smell on her. What was strange was the fact that she had no smell. We'd been smelling ammonia so much that its absence was glaring.

She seemed like she was crying, but when I walked up on her, she acted like nothing was wrong.

"Hey, Ulysses," she said, her voice half cracking. "I'm tired. I'm going to bed."

I could kill Uncle Mike for this.

Seeing her like this was breaking my heart.

It was all bad.

The same went for me and Aisha. It had been over a month since that night at the party. I was damn near stalking her. Whether I bumrushed her at school or hid in the bushes outside of her apartment, she still wasn't feeling me. And for real, I couldn't blame her.

I was a palm tree caught in the Santa Ana winds. My life was on fire, swaying out of control.

Even my relationship with Herc was getting a little tense.

"Man, where you been?" Herc said. "You done missed three parties already. Now you gon' make it four? It's that bitch again, ain't it?"

**SNOOP DOGG**
**and DAVID E. TALBERT**

"Man, fuck you," I said, grabbing his collar, ripping his shirt, backing him up against the wall.

"Nah, nigga, fuck you. Don't be putting your hands on me. I'd punch you in your muthafuckin' mouth if we didn't need it for you to start rappin' again," he said, freeing himself and walking off. "And you owe me a shirt."

He didn't know what was really going on and I couldn't tell him because if I did, I would put him in danger, too.

Everything around me was falling apart.

Just as I was about to walk in the house one night, I could overhear Harvey and Mama yelling.

"What's going on?" I said, racing through the door.

The yelling stopped.

"Ain't nothing going on," Harvey said as my mama turned away. "Just grown folks dealing the way grown folks deal."

"Nah, man, grown or not, you don't be yelling at my mama," I said.

Harvey looked at me, then shot my mama one of the craziest looks I'd ever seen him give her.

"Leave it alone, Ulysses," Mama said.

"But, Mama—"

**Love Don't Live
Here No More**

"Leave it alone." She lowered her head and walked into her room. Harvey chuckled to himself and followed.

"Why you ain't say nothing?" I asked Bing, having made a beeline for our bedroom.

"You ain't been here for me to say nothing," he said. "They're always yelling. Always."

"Yeah, well, the next time they do, you let me know, you hear me? You let me know."

Harvey had intimidated Bing. Damn. Another man had taken my place.

There were still four of us living here, but you see, love didn't live here no more. It had moved out, and Harvey had moved in.

I must have stayed up all night thinking how I was going to fix all the shit that was broken. I needed to take back control of the house.

The night went and the morning came.

"Am I ever going back to school?" Bing asked.

We both knew he was running out of excuses for why he was staying home. He'd already had a stomachache, sore throat, and a migraine. I think one day he was even constipated.

"Just a few more days, man," I replied.

"Okay," he said, "but what's wrong with me today?"

**SNOOP DOGG**
**and DAVID E. TALBERT**

"Diarrhea."

Bing looked at me funny and hopped back in the bed.

It didn't help matters that Mama was at home watching him.

My business had almost shut down. It was hard enough dealing out of Crazy Betty's car, but with the word out that Buddha and Chino were beefing, my usual customers had started keeping their distance. Not that they stopped buying. They just stopped buying from me.

That evening, two of Buddha's boys were gunned down in the front seat of their car. That same night, Buddha returned the favor with three of Chino's men, shot execution style in the alley just two blocks away. It was the craziest shit ever.

"If it's gotta go down, then let it go down," Buddha said, standing in his closet filling a duffel bag full of Glocks and AKs, then pulling out the freshest cream sweatsuit. "You keep your ass in this apartment, at least for a while. You stand too close to the fire, you can't help but get burned."

"Nah, man, I'm not hearing that. I'm not leaving you," I said, following him as he stepped toward the door.

"I need you to listen to what I said," he warned. "Stay the fuck away."

**Love Don't Live
Here No More**

Looking at his eyes, I knew he wasn't backing down, but neither was I. All I needed him to do was think I was staying in the apartment, but I wasn't. As soon as he left out, I was gonna find a way to be right behind him.

Through the peephole, I watched him enter the elevator. The doors opened and closed. I grabbed my bag filled with the two guns he had given me, and started to race down the five flights of stairs, desperately hoping to catch him.

*Fourth floor!*

What else could go wrong? I couldn't even deal with the shit at home for the shit in the streets.

*Third floor!*

I couldn't help Mama and Bing if I was dead, but I couldn't let Buddha down, either. Not after everything he had done for me.

*Second floor!*

*If you man enough to pull it out, be man enough to use it.*

The Glocks clanged inside the bag, bouncing off my thigh as I ran down the stairs.

*First floor!*

Quickly making it down, I cracked the door that led to the garage. I could barely see for the salty sweat burning my eyes. It was dark, except for the flicker of a faulty ceiling light. The smell of urine. Buddha stepped off the elevator, heading straight to his truck, already filled with three of his boys.

The mesh-covered steel sliding garage door slowly opened. The glow of high beams flooded their faces. It was an oncoming car. The back window of Buddha's truck lowered, but it was too late.

A flurry of gunshots rattled one after another. I watched helplessly from a crack in the door.

Buddha was hit. He staggered into his truck. One of his boys jumped out, trying to help him. Bullets emptied into them both.

It was like the bullets were ripping through me. Every round, every *th-th-th-th-th* of the gun. Buddha fell from the truck with his gun in his hand. As he lay there in a pool of his blood, the headlights dimmed. The car door opened.

Chino stepped out.

With his gun pointed, he walked up to Buddha. He reloaded, his eyes locked on Buddha's face. As if there were any more room in his body for bullets, Chino began to fire.

I watched from the shadows, still behind the door.

**Love Don't Live
Here No More**

*"Don't make this shit your life, 'cause when it's over, it's over,"* I remember Buddha saying, thinking it couldn't be over like this.

Not here.

Not now.

I accidentally banged my knee against the door. *Fuck!*

I held my breath. I wondered if anyone noticed the sound. It was silent. Footsteps approached the door.

*If it's gotta go down, then it's gotta go down.*

I loaded my gun, cocked it, and held the trigger.

The knob turned.

The door opened.

**SNOOP DOGG**
and **DAVID E. TALBERT**

Santa Clara County
**LIBRARY**

Renewals:
(800) 471-0991
www.santaclaracountylib.org